THE
SOLSTICE
CUP

RACHEL DUNSTAN MULLER

ORCA BOOK PUBLISHERS

Library and Archives Canada Cataloguing in Publication

Muller, Rachel Dunstan, 1970-
The solstice cup / written by Rachel Dunstan Muller.

ISBN 978-1-55469-017-6

I. Title.

PS8626.U4415S65 2009   jC813'.6   C2008-907306-1

First published in the United States, 2009
Library of Congress Control Number: 2008940980

Summary: On a visit to Ireland, twin sisters are lured into the "Otherworld,"
where a dangerous enchantment threatens to separate them.

Orca Book Publishers gratefully acknowledges the support for its publishing
programs provided by the following agencies: the Government of Canada through
the Book Publishing Industry Development Program and the Canada Council for the
Arts, and the Province of British Columbia through the BC Arts Council
and the Book Publishing Tax Credit.

Cover artwork by Juliana Kolesova
Cover and text design by Teresa Bubela
Typesetting by Christine Toller
Author photo by Bern Muller

ORCA BOOK PUBLISHERS
PO Box 5626, STN. B
VICTORIA, BC CANADA
V8R 6S4

ORCA BOOK PUBLISHERS
PO Box 468
CUSTER, WA USA
98240-0468

www.orcabook.com
Printed and bound in Canada.
Printed on 100% PCW recycled paper.
12 11 10 09 • 4 3 2 1

CHAPTER ONE

Aunt Joan peered out of the tiny kitchen window into the darkness, her stout body bent over the sink. "What on earth is keeping your sister?" she asked. "She promised she'd be back before the sun went down. I'll have to send your uncle out looking for her if she's not back in ten minutes."

"I can go," Mackenzie offered, pushing her chair back from the table.

"No, lass, you sit tight and finish peeling those potatoes," said her great-aunt. "The last thing we need is both of you wandering out there. And on a wild night like this!" She shook her head. "I should never have let her go off alone, not with that leg of hers. Still limping after five years—imagine. Your mother says the doctors have no explanation for it."

Mackenzie had just started on her last potato when Breanne stumbled in through the back door of the stone farmhouse.

"There you are!" Aunt Joan threw down the turnip she'd been scrubbing and rushed to her great-niece. "I was ready to call out the *gardai* on you! Do you have any idea what can happen to a child out in the glens after dark? And a child like you, all alone..."

Ignoring the anger on Breanne's face, she helped her out of her wet jacket. "Look at you," she continued. "You're covered in mud from head to toe! But you're home and safe, and that's what matters. Get those boots off and then wash yourself up while I finish getting tea on the table."

Mackenzie found her twin sister in the front room a few minutes later. Breanne had released her blond hair from its soggy ponytail and was shaking it out in front of the turf fire that crackled in the fireplace.

"You could have told me you were going out," Mackenzie said as she tried to help her sister untangle a knot at the back of her head.

Breanne yanked her hair away. "I didn't want company."

"Come on," said Mackenzie. "We're ten thousand miles from home. Just for once, maybe we could stick together."

"Stick together?" Breanne shot Mackenzie a dirty look. "After what you did at the Christmas dance last week?"

Mackenzie felt her face go red. "You never told me you liked Dylan. Besides, he asked me to dance. I didn't ask him."

"I saw you out there. Every time a song ended and a new one came on, you were like, 'Oh, this is my favorite song.'" Breanne's voice was high and sickly sweet. "It was disgusting."

"Fine. Be like that." Mackenzie dropped into the overstuffed armchair behind her. "Are you trying to punish Aunt Joan for something too? She was really worried when you were so late."

"Why? Was she afraid I wouldn't be able to outrun the banshees with this leg? A 'child like me'!"

"Don't be so touchy," said Mackenzie. "Anything could have happened—we're in a foreign country, after all."

"Foreign country," Breanne snorted. "We're on a sheep farm in Northern Ireland."

Mackenzie watched her sister tug at the knot in her hair. "You went up to the stones, didn't you," she said.

Breanne shrugged. "Maybe. So?"

"You were looking for the ring."

"Don't be retarded," Breanne said. "It's been five years since you tossed it. It's long gone."

"Yeah, well," said Mackenzie, "you shouldn't have gone up there—especially by yourself. We swore we would never go back."

"Oh please," said Breanne contemptuously. "You can't be serious. We were little kids. We were, like, eight years old. I don't even know how you can remember anything that far back."

Aunt Joan called from the kitchen before Mackenzie could respond. "Tea's ready. Come and eat while it's still hot!"

❧

"I don't suppose you hear much about the fair folk in Canada, now do you?" Uncle Eamon asked after they'd finished their evening meal. He pushed his chair away from the cleared table and lit his pipe with fingers that were thick and callused.

Mackenzie shot her sister a warning glance. "The fair folk?"

"Aye, the wee folk, the 'faeries,'" Aunt Joan said as she set a tray of small cakes on the table.

"Uh, no," said Mackenzie. "Not really. Except in kids' books."

"Here in Ireland, we take the fair folk a bit more seriously, especially at this time of year," said Uncle Eamon. "You know what day it is, lass?" he asked Breanne, who was smirking.

Mackenzie answered quickly, before her sister could come up with some sarcastic reply. "Thursday, the twentieth of December."

"Which makes tomorrow the twenty-first," said Aunt Joan. "That's the winter solstice."

"The shortest day of the year," said Mackenzie, ignoring her sister's rolling eyes.

"And one of the most dangerous, if you don't mind yourself." Aunt Joan filled the first of the four cups in front of her with tea. "You don't want to be caught out after dark on the solstice, that's for certain."

Breanne took the teacup from her aunt's hand. "Why not?" she asked. "What do the faeries do on the solstice—set people's hair on fire? Steal babies?"

Uncle Eamon's grizzled chin bobbed up and down. "Aye, 'tis easy to mock the wee folk when you're inside a warm house with the lights on and good company around you. I doubt you'd feel so brave all alone in the glens."

"Seriously." Mackenzie leaned forward. "What happens at the winter solstice?"

"The barrier that separates our world and the world of the fair folk is stretched thin, so it is," Aunt Joan said. Her voice dropped to a dramatic whisper. "Your uncle can tell you a tale or two."

"My sister, your grandmother, was the best story-teller in the family, God rest her soul," said Eamon. "But I'll do the best I can." He took a few puffs from his pipe before beginning the first story.

❧

Mackenzie let herself down carefully onto her collapsible metal cot a few hours later. Breanne was already in bed on the other side of the cluttered sewing room that doubled as a guest room.

"One night down, twelve more to go," Breanne said. "Let's hope they don't go on like that every night. That was so boring, I was ready to stab myself with a fork."

"Shhh—they'll hear you!" Mackenzie whispered. "Besides, I thought it was interesting. I learned some new stuff. Do you realize it was the solstice the last night we were here, five years ago?"

"What are you talking about? We were here in June. We missed the last few weeks of school."

"We flew home on June twenty-third—I remember because it was the day before Mom's birthday," said Mackenzie. "The day before that was June twenty-second. That's the summer solstice, the longest day of the year."

Breanne yawned. "So?"

"So—it's starting to make sense now," said Mackenzie. "What happened up at the stones."

Breanne raised herself up on one elbow. "Why are you so obsessed with that night? *Nothing* happened, Mackenzie, except that I found a ring near the stones, and you were jealous and threw it away. And then you made up some story about an arm reaching up from the shadows to scare me. I would have gone back up to look for the ring the next morning if we hadn't left so early."

"You saw something too," Mackenzie insisted. "I know you did! And what about your leg?" she asked after a pause. "Breanne?"

"I twisted it," her sister said.

"Then why hasn't it healed?"

Breanne flopped down angrily. "Just give it a rest already! We're not little kids anymore."

"Aunt Joan and Uncle Eamon would have known what to do," said Mackenzie. "We should have told them about it back then, but we were too scared."

Breanne snorted. "Too scared they'd laugh at us. You don't think they really buy all that stuff about faeries, do you, Mackenzie? They were just entertaining us tonight. That's what old people do in Ireland after dinner. They sit around telling stories—if they don't have satellite TV, that is."

"They do so believe in faeries," Mackenzie said. "Why do you think there are horseshoes over the doors and iron bars over the windows? To keep the wee folk out."

"Whatever."

"I'm not making this up," Mackenzie said defensively. "Aunt Joan told me all about it. And those thorn bushes in the middle of all the fields we passed on our way here? Those are faery thorns. No one who lives in the glens would ever dare cut down a faery thorn."

Breanne's voice was dripping with sarcasm. "Would someone *please* invite these people into the twenty-first century? I can't believe Mom ditched us here!"

"What was she supposed to do?" said Mackenzie. "Grandpa's dying in the hospital in Belfast. She couldn't leave us in Vancouver while she spent time at his bedside."

"I know, it's very sad. But it's not like we were close to him. We'd only met him a few times. She didn't have to drag *us* halfway around the world," Breanne said. "We could have stayed with friends."

"For two weeks? With Dad long gone and Mom in another country?"

"You are such an old lady, Mackenzie," her sister said angrily. "Why do you always have to take Mom's side? She could have let us stay in Belfast with her. At least then we would have been in a city."

"We're too young to be hanging around Belfast by ourselves," said Mackenzie.

"We're not babies," said Breanne. "We're almost thirteen."

Mackenzie turned out the lamp beside her bed. The cot creaked as she rolled over and tried to find a more comfortable position. "You could try to enjoy yourself, you know. It wouldn't kill you. Uncle Eamon said he'd drive us into the village tomorrow after lunch if we wanted."

"Oh wow!" Breanne's voice rose in mock excitement. "The amazing seaside metropolis of Cushendun! Population, like, seventeen! I can't wait!"

"Fine, stay here then. I'm going to finish my Christmas shopping."

"Cushendun isn't big enough to have any decent stores," said Breanne. "You'll be lucky to find a tourist shop. Hope everyone on your list likes leprechauns and shamrocks."

❧

Breanne was sitting on the hood of Uncle Eamon's Land Rover when Mackenzie came out of the farmhouse after lunch the next day. "If I stay, I have to help Aunt Joan make sandwiches for some stupid church tea," Breanne said with a sullen shrug.

Uncle Eamon came out a moment later, adjusting his tweed cap. "Och, there you are. Doors are unlocked—go ahead, hop in."

The car reeked of wet wool and sheep dung. Out of the corner of her eye, Mackenzie saw her sister wrinkle her nose in disgust as she tried without success to make the seat belt work.

"Don't worry about those," Uncle Eamon said with a wave of his hand. "They don't work."

Fifteen minutes later, he pulled over in the center of Cushendun. "I'm just going up the road a bit to see a friend and have a look at his wee heifer. I'll be back to pick you up by half-four at the latest."

"That's four thirty," Mackenzie translated as the Land Rover pulled away.

"I know what 'half-four' means, thank you," Breanne said. "It means we're stuck here for the next two and a half hours."

Mackenzie looked up and down the narrow road. There wasn't much to see: a gray expanse of water on one side, and a curving line of black and white houses and a few small shops on the other. It looked pretty dreary in the December rain.

"Gee," said her sister. "It's all so overwhelming I don't know where to begin."

"Oh, give it a rest, Breanne," Mackenzie said. She started across the street toward a shop with a display of silk scarves and pottery knickknacks in its window. Her sister followed behind.

"Well, aren't we going in?" Breanne asked impatiently when Mackenzie stopped in the shop doorway. "At least we'll be out of the rain."

Mackenzie stepped aside so her sister could read the handwritten sign taped to the door. The store was only open on Fridays and Saturdays during the winter season. It was Thursday.

"Great," said Breanne. "Now what?"

"There's got to be something else," said Mackenzie. But aside from a few pubs, a small grocery store, a postal outlet and a veterinary office, there wasn't.

"Well, that's it. I'm out of here," Breanne said when they had completed their two-minute survey of the town.

"What are you talking about?" said Mackenzie. "We can't just take off."

"Watch me," Breanne said over her shoulder. She walked away, her left foot dragging a little with each step. "I'm buying a couple of chocolate bars, and then I'm hiking back to the farm."

"And what am I supposed to do, wait here for Uncle Eamon all by myself?" Mackenzie called.

Breanne shrugged. "Stay here, come with me, I don't care. But I'm not hanging around this ghost town all afternoon."

Mackenzie caught up with her sister as she entered the tiny food market at the end of the short main street. "But we have no way of reaching Uncle Eamon. How will he know where we've gone?"

"How long is it going to take him to figure out we're not in Cushendun—maybe five minutes?" said Breanne. "When he can't find us, he'll call Aunt Joan. She'll tell him we're back already, and he'll drive home. Simple." She stopped in front of the candy display next to the till and selected a few chocolate bars. A cashier with a pierced nose accepted her payment without comment.

"We *can't,* Breanne," Mackenzie argued after they'd left the store. "We promised Mom we wouldn't be any trouble for Uncle Eamon and Aunt Joan."

"So what did Eamon expect we were going to do here for two hours?" said Breanne. "Skip stones in the bay?"

"All right, what about the solstice then?" Mackenzie asked, holding her breath.

"What about it?"

"It could be dangerous to go walking through the glens today."

Breanne groaned. "When are you going to grow up, Mackenzie?"

∞❧

"I told you this was a bad idea," Mackenzie said. They'd been walking for forty minutes, and they were still crossing the same boggy field. Mackenzie's not-so-waterproof boots had long since surrendered to the oozing mud. She was soaking wet and covered with slime up to her knees.

"It's not like anyone kidnapped you," Breanne snapped.

"I couldn't just let you take off by yourself," said Mackenzie. "I promised Mom I'd look out for you."

Breanne stopped. "Look out for me? What the heck is that supposed to mean! Did she ask you to?"

"No, but you need someone to watch out for you," said Mackenzie. "You're always taking off, always going on these stupid adventures—like you have to prove yourself or something. Like walking across this bog. It's too much for you!"

"Too much for *me*?" Breanne's hands were on her hips. "You're the one who's been whining about how tired you are for the last half hour!"

"It's *you* I'm worried about," said Mackenzie. "Look at the way your leg is dragging!"

Breanne started marching again. "Don't talk to me about my defective leg, and I won't talk to you about your defective brain," she called back angrily.

"All right, let's change the subject then," Mackenzie said as she picked her way through the mud after her sister. "I know—here's a good question. Do you really know where you're going? Because in case you haven't noticed, there's some fog rolling in, and it's starting to get dark."

"I told you, this is a shortcut. I walked around this area yesterday. The road to the farm should be just over that hill up ahead of us."

Mackenzie stopped again. "The road 'should be' or 'is' over the hill, Breanne?"

"Oh for Pete's sake! It's not like I memorized a map."

"Okay, this is officially completely insane," said Mackenzie. "Time to turn around."

"If it's not over this hill, it's over the next one," Breanne insisted, still walking. "As long as we keep going in a straight line, we'll be fine."

"Or else we'll be completely lost," said Mackenzie. "Come on, Breanne. Breanne!"

"Go back if you want," Breanne called over her shoulder. "Oh, wait, I forgot—you're *afraid* to be out here all by yourself."

A gust of wind caught Mackenzie's ponytail and flicked her in the face. She looked back the way they'd come, and then she turned to stare after her sister. The landscape was gray and empty in both directions.

"I hate you sometimes, you know that?" Mackenzie said as she started walking again.

❧

It was unnerving how quickly the mist swallowed them up. Within minutes Mackenzie could barely make out anything past her own boots and the silhouette of her sister climbing the hill, as if in slow motion, beside her. It wasn't just the lack of visibility slowing them down. It was hard moving through the cold, heavy air. Mackenzie's clothes were damp right through to the skin. With the added moisture, she felt as if she'd gained ten pounds.

"Aren't you worried yet?" Mackenzie asked Breanne. "How are we supposed to find our way back if we can't see anything?"

"Calm down," Breanne said, although her voice sounded tense. "As long as we're walking uphill, we know we're going in a straight line. The fog will clear soon."

"What was that?" Mackenzie asked.

"What?"

"I heard something, some kind of music."

"Like sheep bells?" said Breanne. "Duh! There are sheep all over the place around here."

"Not sheep bells," said Mackenzie. "There it is again! Listen—it *is* music. Don't you hear it?"

"I hear running water," Breanne said after a few seconds. "There must be a stream up ahead of us. Watch where you step."

"There's something more, some kind of weird melody above the sound of the water," Mackenzie insisted. "Now it's gone."

"I didn't hear it," said Breanne. "You've got Uncle Eamon's faery stories on your brain."

They continued moving forward cautiously until they reached the edge of a steep streambed. The mist was thinner where the ground dropped away. A few yards below, Mackenzie saw dark water flowing swiftly downhill before it disappeared into a natural tunnel.

Breanne crouched suddenly. "There's something sparkling down there."

"How can you see anything from up here? Wait, where are you going?" Mackenzie asked as her sister scrambled down the steep bank.

Breanne reached down for something at the edge of the dark water. When she stood up again, she was holding something shiny in her fingers. "Look—it's a ring! It's just like the one I found five years ago!"

"I thought you couldn't remember things clearly that far back," Mackenzie said as she shifted her feet nervously.

"I remember it now," said Breanne. "It was just like this, with a purple stone and all this cool engraving around it. It looks ancient. I bet it's worth a fortune!"

Mackenzie's skin had started to tingle unpleasantly. She stepped back as her sister came up the bank again. "I don't know, Breanne. I have a weird feeling about this. I think you should let it go."

"What do you mean, let it go?" said Breanne. "No way!"

Mackenzie took another step away from the edge of the streambed. "Please, Breanne. Toss it, and let's get out of here!"

"Not this time!"

Breanne had almost reached the top, but at the last second she slipped and had to catch herself. She swore as the ring fell from her hand and bounced down toward the water.

"Leave it," Mackenzie pleaded.

Breanne scrambled backward. "Don't be stupid," she said as she crouched by the edge of the water again. "I let you throw away one ring—I'm not losing this one too." She let out another curse as the ring slipped from her fingers a second time. This time it bounced into the stream.

Before Mackenzie could do anything to stop her, Breanne had removed her jacket and pushed up the sleeves of her sweater. She leaned forward, and her right arm disappeared past her elbow in the water. "Got it. What the—," she yelped.

From where Mackenzie stood, it looked as if something was tugging on her sister's arm. As she watched helplessly, Breanne lost her balance and tumbled forward into the water.

"Breanne!" Mackenzie yelled, sliding down the bank.

The stream was deeper and stronger than it appeared from above. The fast-moving water had already carried Breanne to the edge of the tunnel by the time Mackenzie reached the water's edge. Breanne had managed to grab hold of a small bush that grew next to the opening, but the earth that held the bush was crumbling away.

"Hold on, I'm coming!" Mackenzie cried.

She lunged for her sister a second before the bush came free from the bank. She tried to brace herself as she clung to Breanne's arm, but the force of the water was too much. With nothing to anchor her to the shore, Mackenzie was pulled into the water after her sister.

In an instant, she lost all sense of time, all sense of direction. She couldn't breathe. The icy water was everywhere: in her eyes, in her nose, in her lungs. She tried to fight the current, but it was too strong. Her body grew heavier as the underground river swept her farther and farther from the light. Her mind went as black as the water.

CHAPTER TWO

Something hard rapped against Mackenzie's shoulder. "Wake up. Come on, you're a wee bit wet, but you're not drowned."

Mackenzie's eyes fluttered open. Her brain struggled to make sense of the words she had just heard.

"There, you see? You're not dead yet."

Two pale gray eyes in an ancient wrinkled face came into focus a few feet above Mackenzie's head. "What happened—where am I?" she said as she tried to sit up.

An arm descended to help pull Mackenzie up from the shallow water that lapped around her body. "Gently now. 'Tisn't an easy passage you've just made."

Mackenzie staggered to her feet and looked around, trying to get her bearings in the weak light.

She was ankle-deep in brackish water at the edge of a small reed-covered island. Bulrushes and more reedy islands radiated out in every direction, until they disappeared in the mist.

Mackenzie's focus returned to the tiny, white-haired woman standing beside her. "Poor, waterlogged *bairn*," the old woman said. She removed her cloak and reached up to arrange it around Mackenzie's shivering body. "'Twill have to do until we can get you something dry of your own."

Mackenzie felt more than a little disoriented as she stared back at her rescuer. The old woman was a head shorter than Mackenzie. She was dressed in the most primitive-looking clothes Mackenzie had ever seen outside of a movie or a museum. Her gray tunic was coarsely woven, and the wool cloak she'd spread over Mackenzie's shoulders had been patched so many times that it was almost impossible to see the original fabric. Beneath the water, the woman's feet were bare. In her left hand she gripped a long wooden staff.

"Breanne!" Mackenzie said with a start as her memory returned. "Where's my sister?"

The old woman looked surprised. "There is another one of you?"

"I was trying to pull Breanne out when I fell into the water," said Mackenzie as she looked around anxiously. "She went under just before I did."

The old woman grunted. "Saving your kin is what brought you here, is it? We'd best find her then, before she's found by someone else."

"What do you mean, found by someone else?" Mackenzie asked in alarm. "Where are we?"

"Come," said the old woman. With a wave of her free hand, she started off around the edge of the island. Mackenzie followed her to a raft of crudely lashed boards that had been hidden behind a clump of rushes a few yards away. "We have the advantage," the old woman assured Mackenzie as she motioned her onto the raft. "We know your sister's here."

Mackenzie squatted down near the center of the raft, beside a collection of lidded baskets that smelled strongly of fish. "But where is 'here'? How far did the water carry us?"

"There are some distances that can't be measured, lass." The old woman pushed off from the island using the long staff in her hand. "Not in this world."

"This world?"

"Shhh," said the old woman. "Time for questions later. Be silent now and listen. If we're still, the marsh will tell us where your sister is."

Mackenzie listened, but she heard nothing, not even the faintest breeze. The reeds around them remained motionless. Even the raft made no sound as it drifted through the murky water. Then, as her ears grew accustomed to the silence, she heard a muffled splash some distance ahead.

The old woman tilted her head in the direction of the sound and waited, the end of her staff suspended just above the water. When a second faint splash reached Mackenzie's ears, the old woman nodded and began silently poling the raft toward the source of the distant noise.

Mackenzie peered forward anxiously as the old woman steered the raft around one clump of bulrushes after another. The splashing sounds grew louder and more frequent, and then abruptly they stopped altogether.

"They feel us coming," said the old woman, breaking the silence.

"*Who* feels us coming?" Mackenzie whispered.

"Just the fishies, lass. They're curious creatures. 'Tis the fishies we heard leaping and splashing. They wanted a closer look at the girl lying half in, half above, their world. And there she is," the old woman said as the raft rounded another tiny island.

"Breanne!" Mackenzie called, rising to her feet in relief.

The raft bobbed across the water toward a still figure lying at the base of a clump of reeds. Mackenzie jumped into the shallow water while the raft was still moving forward. She knelt beside her sister and shook her shoulders. "Wake up, Breanne. Come on, wake up!"

Breanne's body twitched and she mumbled something, but her eyes remained closed.

"Open your eyes," said Mackenzie. "We survived— we made it out of the river. Come on, Breanne, wake up!"

"There's some that sleep deeper than others after that journey," said the old woman from behind Mackenzie's shoulder. "Here, crumble a bit of this under her nose."

Mackenzie accepted a skinny bundle of withered-looking leaves. She passed it under her own nose and grimaced.

"It won't hurt her," said the old woman. "They're birthing herbs, but they'll work just as well here. We need to bring her all the way through. Her body's here—it's just her mind that's stuck."

"Stuck where?" Mackenzie asked as she tore off the first leaf and crushed it gingerly under her sister's nose.

"In between," the old woman said. "There, she's found her way."

Mackenzie saw Breanne's nostrils flare, and then her eyes flew open. "What?"

"Oh, thank God," said Mackenzie. "You scared me to death, Breanne!"

"W-what happened?" Breanne asked between chattering teeth as Mackenzie helped her out of the water. "Where are we?"

Mackenzie spread part of the old woman's cloak around her sister's trembling shoulders. "I'm not sure."

"The ring!" her sister said suddenly, dropping down again to feel around in the water by her feet. "I had it in my hand!"

"You won't find it here, that's for certain," said the old woman. "The trap's been sprung; its task is done."

Breanne looked up in surprise. "Who are you?" she demanded.

The old woman cocked her head to the side, like a bird. She made a rapid clicking sound. "That's what they call me here."

"Come again?" said Breanne.

The old woman grinned. "In the common tongue, Maigret of the Marshes."

"Common tongue?" Breanne stood up again with some effort. "What's she talking about, Mackenzie? Where the hell did we end up?"

Mackenzie shrugged. "I told you, I don't know. I've been asking, but the answers don't make any sense."

Breanne turned back to the old woman and spoke slowly, as if she were questioning a young child. "Do you know Joan and Eamon MacHugh? How far are we from their farm?"

Maigret shook her head.

"All right, how about Cushendun? How far are we from Cushendun?"

"Oh, very far, very far," said the old woman.

"Well, we have to get back somehow," said Breanne as her speech returned to its normal pace. "Is there a bus we can catch? A water taxi?"

"Oh no, lass, you can't go back," said Maigret. "The ways are closed for seven days. Longer if you aren't wary."

Breanne shook her head in exasperation. "We can't stay here for a week."

"No, you can't stay here," the old woman agreed. "There's no place to keep hidden out here on the edges. Come. Come," she said, motioning to the raft. "I'll take you to shelter."

Breanne raised her hands. "Hold on. I'm not going anywhere until you tell us exactly where we are."

"Breanne, can I talk to you for a minute?" Mackenzie pulled her sister out of earshot of the old woman.

"This is insane!" Breanne hissed. "We're in the middle of a bog, who knows how many miles away from where we should be, with some whacked old woman who wants to make us her houseguests for a week. It's like something out of some twisted horror movie!"

Mackenzie took a deep breath before whispering, "I know what you're going to say, but I am *not* crazy. Breanne, I don't believe we're in Ireland anymore. At least the Ireland we know. I think when you went after that ring, we were transported somewhere else."

"Somewhere else?" Breanne's eyebrows disappeared under her bangs. "You can't be serious, Mackenzie. You think we're in Faeryland!"

"I don't know where we are exactly," Mackenzie said defensively. "But you heard what the old woman—what Maigret—said. The ring was a trap. We were lured here. It all makes sense."

"What do you mean, we were lured here? We fell into a river and it carried us to this bog! End of story—until Swamp Woman came along."

"You didn't just fall into the river," said Mackenzie. "I was watching. You were pulled in."

"I wasn't pulled in. I slipped!"

"It's not just that," said Mackenzie. "Maigret said the river was some kind of passage—"

"Mackenzie, look at her. Just *smell* her and you can tell she's nuts. She probably escaped from some institution years ago. That's why she's hiding out in this marsh."

"But what if she's not crazy? What if she's telling the truth?"

"Did you hit your head?" Breanne demanded.

"No, I didn't hit my head," Mackenzie said angrily. "Why do I even bother talking to you?"

"Listen," said Breanne. "Here's what we're going to do. We're going back and we're getting on the raft, but only because we don't know any other way out of this swamp. As soon as we get to dry land, we take off and look for a road. We can hitch our way back."

"Fine." Mackenzie crossed her arms. "But in the meantime, let's be nice to Maigret. She's giving us a ride. Besides, we don't know for sure who she is yet."

"She's a crazy woman, Mackenzie," Breanne said. "Not a banshee, not a faery, not a shape-shifter with mystical powers. Just a crazy woman."

Mackenzie followed her sister back to the water's edge. "We'll see," she said under her breath.

CHAPTER THREE

Mackenzie huddled closer to Breanne under the borrowed cloak. They were crouched together in the center of Maigret's raft. The old woman had been silently poling them through the marsh for what seemed like hours. It was impossible to tell how much distance they'd covered. In the dim light, every clump of rushes looked the same.

"For all we know, she's just taking us in circles," Breanne whispered.

"Shhh," said the old woman. "We're getting close now. Best pull that cloak over your heads and keep still until I tell you it's safe."

Mackenzie ignored her sister's protests and pulled the cloak over top of them. "Tell me off later," she whispered as she clamped a hand over her sister's mouth. "But let's just do what she says for now, okay?"

She had to suppress a squeal when Breanne pinched the delicate skin of her forearm. "I'll play along for now," Breanne whispered as soon as her mouth was free. "But I'm calling the police on this crackpot as soon as I get the chance."

Time passed even more slowly in the darkness under the heavy cloak. Mackenzie had created a small opening just beneath their faces, but the air was still thick and stale. She was about to shift her legs, when she heard the old woman begin to sing in a foreign language. There was something in Maigret's voice that told Mackenzie the song was meant as a warning to her and her sister. Even Breanne seemed to feel it. Her body grew tense beside Mackenzie, and she had almost stopped breathing.

Mackenzie held her own breath and listened. Everything was muffled through the wool cloak, but somewhere ahead she heard a strange clicking noise followed by laughter.

"Back from the edges, are you, Maigret?" a man's voice called suddenly from above them. "And what did you catch today?"

Breanne's fingers dug into Mackenzie's wrist. Mackenzie gritted her teeth and prayed that her sister would stay silent.

"Naught to get excited about," the old woman replied. "A basket of eels, a few quail eggs and some herbs to season them."

"Fresh eels," said the voice of a second man. "We shall look for them at tonight's banquet."

Mackenzie listened intently, but the exchange seemed to be over. A few minutes later, the raft bumped into something solid.

"Quickly," the old woman whispered while Mackenzie and Breanne were still trying to regain their balance. She pulled off the cloak and motioned above their heads to a crude shack that stood above the water on stilts. A wooden ladder was lashed to one of the stilts.

Breanne climbed up first, with Mackenzie right behind her. The ladder led through a trapdoor in the shack floor and into a small room that reeked of fish. There were two small paneless windows, which provided just enough light for Mackenzie to make out a pile of baskets and a bundle of wool blankets in one corner of the room and a tall wooden frame with threads strung across it in the opposite corner. There was a stool beside the wooden frame. It was the only piece of furniture visible in the shack.

"'Tisn't the grandest place, but it's safe," the old woman said as she climbed through the trapdoor behind them. "I'll bring you food and drink, and you can stay here until the ways open again in seven nights."

"Wait a minute." Breanne held up her hand. "We need some explanations. What is this 'seven nights' business you keep going on about? What are the 'ways'? Why can't we go back now? And who were those men you spoke with a few minutes ago? Where *are* we?"

Maigret sat down on a tall, lidded basket behind her and folded her wrinkled hands in her lap. "You've passed between worlds, lass. You're in the land below now. The Otherworld."

"What do you mean, the *Otherworld*?"

"The home of the fair folk," said Maigret. "The faerie."

Breanne folded her arms across her chest. "So you're saying you're a faery then."

"Not I," said the old woman. "I'm as mortal as you are."

"Then what are you doing here?" Breanne demanded, one eyebrow lifted.

Maigret shrugged. "A choice I made, many years ago."

"All right then," Breanne said slowly, as if she were humoring a child. "So let's say we really *are* in Faeryland. Why can't we go home now?"

"The ways—the passages between the worlds—open at the winter solstice," said the old woman. "But they are open in only one direction until the solstice feasting is over. That's seven nights hence. You'll be free to leave then, unless—"

"Unless?" said Mackenzie.

The old woman leaned forward. "You were lured here for seven days by a bit of faerie gold. You are a guest here, but that could change if you are not wary."

"I don't believe this," said Breanne, rolling her eyes.

"You'd best believe it, lass," said Maigret, sitting up as tall as her tiny frame would allow. "You'll be safe if you stay here, out of sight."

"And if we don't?" Breanne demanded.

"Seven days could become seven years. And that's seven years in *this* world. No telling how much time would have passed in your world." Maigret rose as she spoke and came toward Breanne. "I noticed you favoring your leg earlier. Were you injured on your way through?"

Breanne's cheeks flushed. "My leg is fine, thank you."

"It happened five years ago," Mackenzie began. The icy look her sister gave her shut her up.

"Five years old, is it? A pity," the old woman said with a shrug. "My herbs could have helped when the injury was new, but there's little they can do for you now. Your blue lips and shivering limbs are another matter. Those I can fix." She turned toward the stack of blankets in the corner. "You'll find new garments in that pile. A little coarser than the ones you're wearing, but they're clean and dry. You'll be wanting some food too." She opened one of the baskets on the floor beside her. "I'll be back when I can with something fresher, but for now here's bread and dried fish to take the edge off your hunger. And there's water in this jug."

"Wait—where are you going?" Breanne asked as the old woman started back down the ladder.

"I've business to take care of on the island," said Maigret. "Don't be frightened. Stay out of sight and no one will bother you while I'm gone. I'll be back before morning."

⁂

"I'm not going to sit here all night, that's for sure," Breanne said after she and Mackenzie had both removed their wet clothes and changed into patched tunics.

Mackenzie removed a chunk of hard bread and a handful of dried fish from one of the baskets in the corner. "Want some?"

"You're kidding, right?"

"Actually, it's not that bad," Mackenzie said after she'd taken a few tentative bites.

"That's disgusting," Breanne said with a grimace. "I can't believe you put that stuff in your mouth."

"I'm hungry. We're going to need to eat something if we're stuck here for a week."

"We're not going to be stuck here for a week," said Breanne. "C'mon, Mackenzie, even you can't be that gullible! Hey—quit chewing for a second," she said suddenly. "I heard something."

Mackenzie listened with her sister, her muscles tensing. "It's music. It's the same music I heard before in the fog."

"But where's it coming from?" Breanne asked as she pushed herself to her feet and went to one of the small windows.

"Stop!" Mackenzie whispered. "What if someone sees you?"

"Oh, please. You don't really buy all that stuff about faeries, do you?" Breanne asked. "The old woman just wants company over the holidays. I bet we're the only visitors she's had in years. No wonder, if she really lives in this hovel."

"Please, Bree. Be careful!"

"Calm down—no one can see me," Breanne assured her sister. "Come look for yourself. There's land over there. I bet we could wade to shore. The water can't be very deep if the old woman can move her boat around with a pole."

Mackenzie crept toward the window. It had gotten darker since they'd entered the shack, but the land facing them was still visible as a low black mound dotted with twinkling lights. Some of the lights appeared to be moving, as if they were flashlights or lanterns.

"Listen," said Breanne. "That's laughter and people singing. They're having some kind of party over there."

"What are you doing?" Mackenzie asked.

Breanne had returned to the center of the room and was pulling on her boots. "Are you kidding me?" she said as she balled up the wet clothes she'd removed earlier and stuffed them into an empty basket. "There are *people* over there! People who can help us get back to the farm. Not that I'm in a hurry to get back, but Aunt Joan has probably got the whole Irish army looking for us by now. Come on, grab your clothes!"

Mackenzie shook her head. "I'm staying."

"What do you mean, you're staying?"

"I think we should wait here, like Maigret told us to."

"Are you *crazy*?" Breanne stared in disbelief at her sister. "You can't be serious. What if she puts a lock on the trapdoor when she comes back? This is our chance to get away!"

"I'm not crazy!" Mackenzie replied angrily. "But if we'd waited for Uncle Eamon like I wanted to, we wouldn't be here! And we wouldn't be here either if you hadn't made us keep walking into the fog, or if you hadn't gone after that stupid faery ring!"

"*Faery* ring," Breanne said in disgust. "You seriously believe that psycho?"

"Well, what if she's telling the truth?"

Breanne's entire head rolled back with her eyes this time. "I can't believe we're having this conversation. Get real, Mackenzie. We're lost, but we're not in Faeryland!"

"I don't care what you say this time. I'm staying," said Mackenzie.

"Fine." Breanne opened the trapdoor. "It's not like I can drag you across the water. I'll send someone to get you as soon as I can."

The shack seemed to get darker the instant Breanne disappeared down the ladder. Mackenzie waited a few seconds and then called down softly, "Breanne?"

There was a faint splash. "I'm down," said Breanne. "Throw me my basket of clothes."

"Wait," said Mackenzie. "I really don't think we should be separated."

"Are you coming then?"

Mackenzie clenched her hands. "I don't know—"

"Well, make up your freakin' mind! I'm up to my waist in freezing water."

"All right, all right—I'm coming."

"Get your clothes then," said Breanne. "We're not coming back."

Mackenzie quickly wrapped some bread, a few dried fish and a small jug of water in a scrap of cloth she found at the bottom of a basket. She stuffed the bundle into the basket with her wet clothes and started down the ladder.

With every step they took toward the illuminated shoreline, Mackenzie's heart beat a little faster. The music coming from the island made her feel strangely light-headed. Even the air was different the closer they got to land. It was thicker, and it left a sickly sweet aftertaste in her mouth.

"This is wrong, Breanne," Mackenzie whispered when they were only a few dozen yards offshore. "Can't you feel it? It's like a giant magnet is pulling us in. Let's go back, before it's too late."

"Too late for what?" Breanne said. "This is cool! Someone's having an awesome party over here, and we get to crash it!"

Mackenzie stopped. "Just this once, listen to me," she begged. "We're in way over our heads this time."

Breanne was still wading forward. She didn't respond.

"Please, Breanne, what about Maigret's warning?"

"What about it?" Breanne said with a dismissive laugh. "I'm not going to sit in a dirty shack for a week and miss this. This is like something from a dream!"

"Or a nightmare," Mackenzie said as her sister continued moving toward the shore. "Wait, Breanne. Wait!"

Breanne looked over her shoulder. "Don't you ever get tired of being such a wuss, Mackenzie? Go back and hide if you want to. I'm going to have some fun."

"Please, Bree!"

Mackenzie held her breath for a few seconds. The water rippled around her as she started moving forward again.

CHAPTER FOUR

Mackenzie stepped out of the water a few seconds after her sister. She let the borrowed tunic she'd been holding above her waist fall back to her ankles.

"All right, we're here," she whispered through clenched teeth. "What's next, according to your great plan?"

Breanne hid her basket in a recess between two small boulders at the foot of a tall stone wall. "Now we check out the party."

"I can't believe I'm doing this," Mackenzie muttered, trying to ignore the tightening in her chest. She rummaged in her own basket until she found the small bundle that held the food and water she'd grabbed from Maigret's shack. She slipped the bundle down the front of her bulky tunic and retied her belt.

It was awkward, but it allowed her to keep both hands free. When she was satisfied that the provisions were secure, she hid her basket beside her sister's.

"Come on, over here," Breanne beckoned.

Mackenzie followed her sister to the base of a steep staircase, dimly lit by torches. She looked up and shook her head. "I can't do it."

"What do you mean, you can't do it?" Breanne said. She was already on the fifth stair.

"I mean this is the stupidest thing you've ever done, and I'm not following you anymore."

"Oh, whatever," said Breanne. "I'm sick of listening to you whine."

Mackenzie watched her sister drag her left leg after her right one up the stairs. Breanne hesitated for a second at the top and then disappeared.

"She didn't even turn around," Mackenzie muttered in disbelief. She waited for a few moments, willing her sister to reappear at the top of the steps. When the stairs remained empty, she looked back toward the water. Maigret's shack wasn't visible in the dark. "I hate you sometimes, Breanne!"

Mackenzie took a deep breath and forced herself to start climbing. Her heart nearly stopped when a hand reached for her at the top of the stairs.

"It's only me," Breanne whispered as she pulled Mackenzie into a dark alcove. "I can't believe it—look! It *is* Faeryland!"

Mackenzie stared openmouthed at the scene in front of them. Illuminated by flickering yellow torches, a procession of masked merrymakers leapt and spun down an avenue lined with leafless trees. The dancers seemed to grow and shrink and even change shape as they moved in and out of the shadows. Mackenzie caught glimpses of hooves, antlers and giant wings. Everything was in motion. She felt dizzy just watching the flickering scene.

Mackenzie stepped back against the stone wall behind her and tried to catch her breath. "All right, we've seen it—can we please go now?"

"We're not exactly dressed for this party, are we?" said Breanne, raising a hand to her wet hair.

"Not exactly," Mackenzie said, her voice strained. She grabbed her sister's arm. "Come on, let's get out of here."

"I was kidding," Breanne said. "Who cares what we look like? We're never going to get another chance like this!"

Before Mackenzie could react, Breanne wrenched her arm away and launched herself into the teeming crowd. The dull fabric of her tunic disappeared almost instantly in the sea of exotic colors.

"Breanne!" Mackenzie called. Her voice was lost in the music and the clamor of the dancing throng. With no time to think, she leaped after her sister.

It was like falling back into the dark river that had swept them underground. The dancers surged forward, and Mackenzie was carried along with them, past the spot where she'd last seen Breanne. She heard a strange hissing, clicking chorus rise around her. Bony fingers poked and prodded her body. Terrified, she tried to fight her way back to the edge of the crowd.

A hand closed around her arm before she could escape. "You look lost," a voice purred in her ear.

The world around her stopped spinning long enough for Mackenzie to turn and look into the face of a tall, slender young woman in a shimmering cloak. Her skin was so pale it was almost blue, and she had large silver eyes. Mackenzie was sure the woman was a faery.

Her arm tingled unpleasantly under the faery woman's fingers. She tried to pull away, but the faery's grasp was firm.

"Trust me, this is no place for a human child by herself," she said. "I'm not going to hurt you. I'm taking you somewhere quiet where we can introduce ourselves properly." She didn't wait for a reply. The current that had been too strong for Mackenzie didn't seem to exist for her. Mackenzie didn't protest as the faery dragged her through the throng.

"Much better," the faery said when they had reached the edge of the crowd and turned onto a quieter path. "Now tell me your name, and you'll be under my protection."

Mackenzie hesitated.

"Quickly!" the faery said impatiently, squeezing Mackenzie's arm. "I can't keep you safe without it. You're lucky I was the first to find you. There are Pookas around that would swallow your soul as soon as look at you."

"My name—" Mackenzie swallowed. "My name is Mackenzie."

"Is that it? Is that the whole thing?"

Mackenzie shook her head. "It's Mackenzie Brooke Howell."

"Mackenzie Brooke Howell," the faery repeated carefully, her eyes glittering. Her lips curled up in an almost feline smile of satisfaction. "You can call me Nuala, Mackenzie. We're going to have fun together, you and I! But you must be tired and hungry if you've just arrived." Her gaze moved down to Mackenzie's tunic. "And you can't be comfortable in that ugly thing. Come with me. We'll find you something much nicer."

Mackenzie looked over her shoulder anxiously. "But my sister—I lost her back there somewhere. I need to find her."

"You have a sister here as well?" Nuala tilted her head, as if considering how to use this information. "A pity you didn't tell me right away," she said with a shrug. "Someone else will have claimed her by now." She tugged at Mackenzie's arm. "Come on, let's go."

"But I can't go anywhere," said Mackenzie, her voice climbing. "What if one of those things that swallows souls has Breanne? I need to find her... ouch!" Mackenzie stopped abruptly, startled by a sudden burning sensation where the faery's fingers held her arm. Her skin felt as if it had brushed against a stinging nettle plant.

Nuala's eyes had lost their shimmer. "There's no need to get hysterical. I'm sure your sister is fine. Now—you're tired and hungry, aren't you?" she asked calmly.

Mackenzie's heart was lodged in her throat. "A—a little," she whispered.

"Good. Then follow me."

❧

The music and noise got fainter as Nuala led Mackenzie down a long, torch-lit path lined with leafless trees and thorn bushes. More than once Mackenzie was sure she heard someone following them, but when she turned her head she saw only shadows. Tiny bells on Nuala's slippers jangled with every step. The faery hummed softly as they walked, a melancholy tune that made Mackenzie feel even more uneasy.

"Through here," the faery said at last.

They'd come to a tall stone archway at the end of the path. Beyond the arch, Mackenzie saw a low mound silhouetted against the night sky. A wide set of stone stairs descended into the ground at the base of the mound.

Mackenzie felt a prickling sensation run through her body as Nuala led her under the arch. Then they were on the stairs, going down into the earth. They passed under another stone arch and entered a corridor dimly lit by more torches. Mackenzie was surprised by the size of the corridor. It was wide enough for a dozen people to walk side by side, and long enough that she couldn't see where it ended. More passages branched off from both sides of the corridor.

Mackenzie tried to fix the route they took in her mind, but after the sixth or seventh turn she knew she was lost. In the flickering light, every passage looked the same. Nuala stopped several times to speak with other faeries along the way, conversing in the strange language of hisses and clicks that Maigret had used when she'd first told them her name. Mackenzie could feel the faeries' eyes on her as she turned her own gaze to the floor.

The passages got narrower as they continued on, deeper and deeper underground. Mackenzie started having trouble breathing at the thought of so much earth above her. Nuala finally stopped in front of an open doorway and motioned Mackenzie to enter.

"Go on—it's a guest chamber, not a dungeon," the faery said when Mackenzie hesitated. "No need to look so petrified."

Mackenzie's breath came more easily once she was through the door. Aside from the absence of windows, there was nothing cave-like or subterranean about the room. It was spacious and brighter than the passage outside, thanks to two large candle chandeliers hanging from the ceiling. Floral tapestries covered the walls. Brightly colored rugs hid most of the polished stone floor. There was a canopy bed in one corner of the room, and a large tub just visible behind a screen in the other corner.

"See?" said Nuala, turning in the center of the room. "Isn't it nice? Once you've had a bath and changed into something pretty, I'm sure you'll feel more relaxed."

As if on cue, two silent girls appeared in the doorway, their faces half hidden under the gray hoods of their robes. One of them motioned for Mackenzie to remove her tunic so she could bathe in the tub peeking out from behind the screen. Mackenzie moved behind the screen before disrobing, taking care to keep the bundle of food she'd brought from Maigret's shack hidden from view. The tub was already full of warm scented water, as if Mackenzie's arrival had been anticipated. When her bath was finished, one of the girls produced a white gown of gauzy fabric that seemed to float just above Mackenzie's skin when she slipped it on. As a finishing touch, the second girl wove tiny white flowers into her hair.

Mackenzie stood in the center of the room and waited while Nuala appraised her attendants' work. "Very good," the faery said. She made a clicking noise with her tongue and waved her hand, and the girls curtsied and backed out of the room. "You look very pretty now that you've been cleaned up," Nuala said when they were gone. She sounded pleased. "You may even be the prettiest guest at our banquet tonight."

"Is there a chance my sister will be there?" Mackenzie asked hesitantly.

"Of course," said the faery. "We always bring our guests to the solstice feasts. Our celebrations wouldn't be the same without you."

Mackenzie held her breath as the faery moved closer. She tried not to flinch when Nuala raised a hand to touch one of the flowers in her hair. "You have beautiful skin," Nuala said. "It's almost as pale as mine. Promise you'll stay close to me tonight. We wouldn't want anyone else to steal you away, now would we?"

The faery laughed at the color rising in Mackenzie's cheeks. "You're so young—I *am* going to have fun with you. But I need to leave you alone for a while," she said, letting her hand fall again. "I have to get ready myself. I'll have some food sent in while I'm gone."

"I-I'm not hungry," Mackenzie lied, praying that her stomach would remain silent.

"Really?" The faery tilted her head. "I'm always hungry. But suit yourself. Just as long as you have an appetite tonight."

Mackenzie listened as the bells on Nuala's slippers got fainter and finally faded away altogether. When she was sure it was safe, she retrieved the bundle of food she'd hidden behind the screen. She took a few sips from the water jug and crammed a handful of dried fish and bread into her mouth.

"I can't believe you're still eating that stuff."

Mackenzie almost choked as she spun toward the doorway. "Breanne! Where have you been?" she demanded when she could speak again. "How could you just take off on me like that?"

Breanne undid the clasp of an iridescent cloak like the one Nuala had worn in the street, removing it from her shoulders as she entered the room. "Seriously— they must have better food on this side of the water. Why are you eating moldy fish?"

"Don't you remember the stories Mom used to read to us when we were little?" said Mackenzie. "It's dangerous to eat faery food. Besides, the fish isn't moldy."

"Whatever," Breanne said as she collapsed across the canopied bed.

"Where did you get that cape?" Mackenzie asked suspiciously.

"I found it," said her sister.

"You found it? What, was it just lying in the street?"

"Don't get hysterical," said Breanne. "Some faery chick was spinning it above her head, and when she let go, I caught it."

"You caught it? You mean you stole it!"

"C'mon, I needed *something* to wear over this ugly potato sack. Besides, it's the perfect disguise. With the hood up, I can go anywhere. Which is how I was able to trail *you* without being noticed."

Mackenzie took a deep breath to calm herself. "All right. You followed me, and you're here now—so I'll forgive you for taking off in the first place. Now let's get out of here!"

Breanne made herself more comfortable on the bed. "Why? You've got a good thing going here. A nice room, clean clothes, and didn't I hear something about a banquet tonight? Let's make this our base until the 'ways open' or whatever's supposed to happen in a week. It sure beats that old woman's smelly shack."

Mackenzie stared at her sister in disbelief. "We can't stay here—that's insane! It's way too dangerous!"

Breanne shrugged. "How dangerous can it be? It's not like you're locked up in here. You're a guest—free to come and go."

"Oh, I'm a guest, am I?" Mackenzie rubbed her arm where Nuala had gripped her. "That faery *stung* me when I wanted to stay back and look for you!

And then she said I'd better stick close to her at this banquet tonight so nobody tries to steal me away!"

"Whatever," Breanne said. "If this really is Faeryland, all we have to do to stay out of trouble is be polite. As long we say please and thank you, we'll be fine. That's what all the old faery stories say."

"Be polite?" said Mackenzie. "Be polite? You just stole a cloak from them! Who knows what they'll do to us when they find out!"

Breanne took the cloak and stuffed it under the nearest pillow. "There, no one will ever know. Now chill, before you hyperventilate."

The sound of a collision just outside the room prevented Mackenzie from responding.

"Clumsy slattern!" a man cursed as Mackenzie peered anxiously around the open doorway. "Big-footed wench!"

A redheaded girl, dressed in gray like the girls who had attended Mackenzie, was crouched on the ground beside a young bearded man in a velvet cape. The caped man was kneeling over a set of primitive-looking bagpipes.

"You've broken the chanter," he said angrily. "What do you say to that?"

The trembling girl said nothing.

"Damn it—a piece is missing. I'll tell you what," the man said. "If I can't play tonight, it will be you that answers for it! Now where is that blessed thing?"

Mackenzie teetered off balance as her sister pushed past. Breanne scanned the scene quickly and then bent down over a shallow crevice in the floor. When she stood up again, she was holding a hollow piece of wood in her fingers. "Is this what you're looking for?"

The young man's head swiveled in Breanne's direction. "That's it," he said curtly, reaching up for the piece of wood.

Breanne pulled her hand away. "Didn't anyone ever teach you any manners? You owe her an apology."

The caped man looked as startled by Breanne's words as Mackenzie felt. "What?"

"You were a jerk to her," said Breanne, nodding to the girl still crouched on the floor. "If you want this back, tell her you're sorry."

The man shook his head. The surprise on his face melted into sour amusement. "If that's the price to make my pipes whole again, I suppose I have no choice."

He rose to his feet. When he was standing, Mackenzie saw that one of the man's shoulders was significantly higher than the other, and there was a small hump on his back that had been obscured by the folds of his cloak. He didn't look the least bit repentant, but he made an elaborate flourish with his free arm and bowed toward the cowering servant. "If my temper has given any offense, I do hereby apologize. Is that satisfactory?" he asked, turning back to Breanne.

"It'll do," said Breanne. She seemed less confident now that she'd noticed the man's deformity. She handed him the piece of wood without meeting his eyes.

"Thank you," the caped man said with another bow.

Mackenzie waited until the man's attention was back on his damaged instrument before grabbing her sister by the arm. "I can't believe you just did that!" she hissed as she tried to haul Breanne back through the doorway. "'Be polite,' you said. You can't talk to people like that here!"

"At least one of you has some sense," the man muttered as he continued to inspect his pipes. "She'd be one unhappy lassie now if I'd been one of the fair folk."

"I knew he wasn't a faery," Breanne said to Mackenzie, her cockiness returning. She threw off her sister's hand. "He doesn't have weird eyes or see-through skin like the rest of them. He's human, like us."

"That I am," said the man. He pointed his chin at the retreating back of the hooded serving girl. "So is she, for that matter. You want to take care that you don't end up like her."

"What do you mean?" Mackenzie asked anxiously.

The bearded man tucked his pipes under his arm and surveyed the sisters. "I suppose the end of my chanter is worth a bit of counsel. Fine. Here it is: Beware the solstice cup."

"The 'solstice cup'?" said Breanne. "What's that?"

But the piper had already turned his back on them. He moved away in the direction the servant had taken and didn't turn when Breanne called after him.

"Shh," said Mackenzie. "Listen—I hear bells. Nuala must be coming back."

"All right, already," Breanne said angrily as Mackenzie tugged her out of the corridor. "You don't have to pull my arm off."

CHAPTER FIVE

The silver-eyed faery entered the room with two attendants behind her. Her shimmering cloak was gone. In its place she wore a long dress that seemed to consist entirely of white rose petals. Tiny glowing stones dangled from the brown curls piled up on her head. She halted at the sight of Breanne lounging at the end of the canopied bed beside Mackenzie.

"My sister, Breanne," Mackenzie said nervously, nudging Breanne to stand up.

"Your sister!" the faery repeated, bringing her hands together in satisfaction. "Hasn't anyone else claimed you yet? Then tell me your full name and I'll be your protector," she said when Breanne shook her head.

Breanne surprised Mackenzie by making a small curtsy. "Breanne Caitlin Howell."

Nuala's eyes shone as they went back and forth between the two girls. "You're not just sisters, you're twins! Come closer." She beckoned to Breanne. "Let me see you in the light."

"Is there something wrong with your leg?" the faery asked as Breanne stepped under the nearest candle chandelier.

Breanne's cheeks reddened slightly. "It's nothing. I twisted my ankle, and it hasn't healed yet."

"Hmm. A pity." Nuala looked Breanne up and down and then beckoned to her attendants. "Twins—it's almost too good to be true. I definitely want them to match for the banquet tonight. You'll have to work quickly to get this one ready in time."

Mackenzie expected her sister to protest as the nearest hooded girl approached to help her remove her coarse tunic. But for once, Breanne was as meek as a lamb.

❧

Mackenzie and Breanne had to hurry to keep up with Nuala as she led them away from their chamber a short while later. The two hooded attendants followed behind the sisters.

Breanne ran her hands over her dress and shook her head. "This is a ridiculous outfit," she mouthed behind the faery's back. "They have no fashion sense."

Nuala turned a corner ahead of them while Mackenzie was frowning and holding her finger to her lips. Two turns later, they were in a wide hallway crowded with elaborately dressed faeries, all traveling in the same direction.

"They sound like a bunch of crickets," Breanne muttered to Mackenzie under cover of the din.

"Honestly, Breanne!" Mackenzie hissed through gritted teeth. "You're going to get us in trouble!"

Nuala slowed to let the sisters catch up. "Stay close," she told them. "I don't want you to get swept away."

It was hard to be sure with so many bodies pressing in around them, but it seemed to Mackenzie that they had started to climb toward the surface. Her guess was confirmed when they passed through an ornately carved doorway the height of a two-story house and found themselves in a courtyard above ground. Tiny orbs of light floated above their heads. Beneath the lights, the banquet guests were taking their places at long tables set with jeweled cups and crystal dishes. Servants in gray hoods scurried between the tables, carrying large pitchers and platters of food.

"Quickly," Nuala said, taking Mackenzie and Breanne by the sleeves. "Our seats are waiting. I don't want to miss the first course."

Nuala led the sisters to a table across the courtyard. Most of the seats were already occupied. Mackenzie couldn't help staring at a faery wearing a small bird-cage on a chain around her neck, with a tiny live bird inside. The faery sitting beside her had fluttering butterflies all over her hair, while one of the male faeries had a subdued fox reclining over his shoulder.

A servant waiting on the other side of the table curtsied and pulled out a throne-like chair for Nuala. She pulled out two slightly simpler ones near the end of the table for Mackenzie and Breanne.

"Aren't my guests beautiful," Nuala said proudly to the others at the table before taking her seat. She had the sisters each turn around so they could be admired.

"I'm having trouble breathing," Mackenzie whispered after Nuala had abandoned them to have a conversation in her own language. "They're *still* staring at us. It's creepy!"

"Relax," said Breanne. "I'm sure they'll lose interest in us once the food comes. Hey, look—another girl dressed like an underage bride."

Four tables away, there was a girl dressed in the same type of gauzy white gown that Mackenzie and Breanne were wearing.

"She looks human," said Breanne. "And there's another one. And a guy in a white tunic over there."

"Nuala said there would be other guests like us," said Mackenzie. "I wonder if they got here the same way we did."

"Let's go ask," Breanne said, pushing her chair out.

Mackenzie grabbed her sister's arm. "Breanne—you can't just take off. Nuala specifically told us to stay with her!" She glanced anxiously at the silver-eyed faery, who was still turned away from them, engaged in conversation with a creature who had curled ram's horns growing out of his temples.

"You're such a baby." Breanne shrugged her arm free. "All right, I'll wait. The food's here anyway."

Mackenzie clenched her hands in her lap and tried not to look at the puddings, jellies and tiny pastries that were being set down on the table.

"This is going to be good." Breanne picked up a serving spoon and began filling her plate with food.

"You're not going to eat that, are you?" Mackenzie whispered in dismay.

"Why not?"

"Because you can't eat faery food! Weren't you paying any attention? Just wait, and you can have some of the stuff I brought from Maigret's shack."

Breanne rolled her eyes. "I'm not eating any of that crap." She raised a spoonful of soup to her mouth and swallowed. "Mmm, delicious. And oh, look! I'm still breathing."

Mackenzie stared straight in front of her, too frustrated to speak.

"I don't know what your problem is," Breanne said.

"Look, all the other human guests are eating too. No one's keeled over yet."

"Why don't you ever listen to me?" said Mackenzie. "Why do you always have to ignore everything I say?"

"Because you're a paranoid Goody Two-shoes."

Mackenzie dug her nails into her palms. "Fine. Just wait until you wake up tomorrow and you're paralyzed—or a lizard or something."

Mackenzie still hadn't tasted any of the faery food by the time dessert was brought out.

"You have no idea what you're missing," Breanne said, her mouth full of pastry. "This is *so* good. Come on, try a bite." She lifted her fork toward Mackenzie's mouth. "You know you want to."

Mackenzie turned her head away quickly. "Stop it!"

Breanne giggled as the piece of pastry fell into Mackenzie's lap. She reloaded her fork and tried again. "C'mon, just a little nibble, a teeny-weeny nibbly."

"You're acting like you're drunk!" Mackenzie hissed.

"I'm not drunk," Breanne said indignantly. "I'm just having a good time. You should try it. Hey, look. There's that hunchbacked piper guy."

The bearded man they'd met outside their chamber had just appeared in the center of the courtyard with his pipes nestled under one arm. "Oh goody—he's going to play for us," Breanne said. "Guess his chanter-thingy is fixed."

Mackenzie tried to tune her sister out as she focused on the piper. He settled himself on a stool and brought the chanter to his mouth. At the sound of the first notes, the noise level around the courtyard dropped dramatically. A few servants moved between the tables, removing dishes and refilling cups, while the piper adjusted the instrument under his arm. They slipped away as soon as he was ready to play, and the hall fell completely silent.

The music began quietly, each note an autumn leaf drifting to earth. Mackenzie forgot about her anger at Breanne as she listened. The piper was telling a story with his instrument: of storm clouds gathering on the horizon, of a red sun sinking in the west. As the music got louder, Mackenzie tasted rain on her tongue and felt the wind whip her face.

The notes came harder, faster. Seasons collided; the moon waxed and waned. Mackenzie was a ship tossed on an angry ocean. She was a seed buried deep beneath the ground. She was a snowflake. She was a sheet of ice. She was a dying star in an empty sky.

Time stopped; the courtyard disappeared. And still the piper played on.

Mackenzie had no idea where she was when the last note finally died away. It was as if she'd woken up in some strange underwater world. She blinked, and the figure approaching her slowly came into focus. It was Nuala, her silver eyes gleaming as she held up a two-handled cup. The liquid inside was luminescent.

"Drink," the faery whispered.

Mackenzie took the cup with both hands. It was cold to the touch. She stared, mesmerized, at the glowing white liquid.

"Drink," the faery repeated, her voice a soft purr.

Mackenzie lifted the cup to her mouth.

A loud crash startled her out of her dazed state before the liquid reached her lips. The floating lights that had illuminated the courtyard earlier were gone, but torches still burned on several nearby pillars. Mackenzie was able to make out the misshapen back of the piper crouched near an overturned stool several yards away.

"Drink," Nuala repeated. There was a hint of impatience in her voice this time.

Mackenzie looked at the faery and then at the cup in her hands. "Please—I'm sorry—I can't," she whispered, afraid to lift her eyes. She trembled as the cup was taken from her.

Nuala had moved when Mackenzie looked up again. She stood in front of Mackenzie's sister, holding the cup out for Breanne to take. Breanne's eyes were open, but her expression was vacant.

Mackenzie held her breath as her sister accepted the cup. "Don't," Mackenzie begged silently, shaking her head.

Breanne's eyes remained unfocused as she lifted the cup. Halfway up she stopped, as if she'd forgotten what she was doing. The cup in her hands didn't move; Nuala raised her own hands to guide it toward Breanne's mouth.

"Breanne, no!" Mackenzie whispered. With no time to think, Mackenzie lunged for the cup. She stumbled, and the cup flew from Breanne's hand and clattered to the ground a few yards away. The liquid poured out in a faint glowing trail across the stone floor.

"What's going on?" Breanne said groggily, as Nuala made an angry hissing noise.

Mackenzie barely heard her sister. Her attention was fixed on Nuala's face.

Nuala returned Mackenzie's gaze with eyes that had turned a steely gray. Without looking away, she pointed to the cup and said something in her own language. At the edge of her vision, Mackenzie saw a servant step forward to retrieve it.

"You must be very tired now," Nuala said in a voice without emotion. "My attendants will see you back to your chamber. Sleep tight. I'll see you in the morning."

CHAPTER SIX

Mackenzie's heart accelerated when she woke up in the canopy bed and remembered where she was. "Breanne," she whispered. Her sister continued to snore. "Breanne," Mackenzie said a little louder, rising on one elbow to shake her sister's shoulder.

"What?" Breanne mumbled. "Ouch—stop it!"

"Are you all right? Breanne, talk to me!"

Breanne turned her head and half opened one eye. "Is room service here yet?"

"How can you be so calm?" Mackenzie asked, her voice rising. "This isn't a hotel! We're trapped here! And we almost drank from that cup last night!"

"You're getting hysterical again," Breanne said. "What cup?"

Mackenzie struggled to get her voice under control.

"The cup the guy with the pipes warned us about. The solstice cup!"

"I don't know what you're talking about. I don't remember any cup last night." Breanne rolled over. "Is that your stomach? For Pete's sake, Mackenzie, find something to eat!"

The bundle that held Mackenzie's smuggled food was still in the corner where she'd left it. She tried not to think of the previous night's feast as she took out the two remaining fish and the last crust of bread. The food was gone in a few bites, but not her hunger. Mackenzie's stomach was still growling when one of the gray-hooded attendants appeared in the doorway with a covered tray.

"Mmm, now *that* smells good," Breanne said as she sat up in bed. "Bring that tray right over here."

The servant set the tray down on a table beside the bed and backed out of the room without speaking.

"Now this is what I call breakfast," Breanne said enthusiastically.

Mackenzie frowned as she watched her sister dig into a bowl of berries and cream.

"Oh, get over it," Breanne said, looking back at her sister. "I ate like a pig last night, and I'm fine. There's nothing wrong with the food."

"You were acting like you were drunk at the banquet."

Breanne shrugged. "So I had a little too much of the fruit punch."

Mackenzie clenched and unclenched her hands. Her stomach rumbled as the berries disappeared.

"Mmm. This is even better than what I had last night," Breanne said as she bit into a large pastry.

"All right," Mackenzie said irritably. She stomped across the room and lunged for the remaining pastry. "You don't have to eat it all."

The food was good. In fact it was better than any other meal Mackenzie could remember eating. The pastry was gone in a few melt-in-your-mouth bites. So were the potato cakes and the tiny fried sausages.

"Hey, what are you doing?" she asked suddenly, her mouth full of berry pudding.

Breanne had retrieved the iridescent cloak she'd stuffed under her pillow the day before. "I'm going exploring," she said as she fastened the clasp at her neck. "I want to find the people dressed like us at the banquet last night. The other humans."

Mackenzie dropped her bowl back on the tray. "Wait, Breanne—you can't just take off."

"Why not? The door's open."

"But we need to ask permission!"

"Why?" Breanne looked genuinely surprised.

Mackenzie edged around her sister to block the door. "Please, Breanne. If you'd seen Nuala's eyes when I knocked that cup out of your hands—you've got to stay until she comes!"

Breanne pushed her sister aside. "You stay here and be the good girl. I'm going for a walk."

"But what do I tell her?" Mackenzie asked as her sister disappeared through the doorway. "Bree! Breanne!"

❧

Mackenzie tried to come up with an excuse for her sister's absence while she waited for Nuala, but as she grew more anxious it became harder to think clearly. Her whole body was as tight as a violin string by the time the faery finally appeared in the doorway with two of her attendants behind her.

"What's wrong?" The faery looked around the room. "Where's your sister?"

Mackenzie shook her head. Her voice was strained. "She went out for a walk. I told her we should wait for you..."

Nuala's expression darkened. She said something in her own language, and one of the hooded girls curtsied and backed out of the room. "Didn't I warn you to stay close?" she said in an irritated voice to Mackenzie. "I can't protect the two of you if you're off wandering the corridors by yourselves."

"But I didn't—I tried—"

"Oh well. There's nothing to be done about it at this point," the faery sighed. She waved her hand as if she was already bored with the subject. "I'm sure we'll find your sister before a Pooka gets her. Now—look at the pretty gowns I brought!"

The remaining attendant was already advancing with one of the white dresses. It was similar to the one Mackenzie had worn the night before, but with tiny pearls sewn all over it and a more voluminous skirt. "Isn't it exquisite?" said Nuala. "Quickly, put it on and then we'll do your hair."

The faery's servant positioned a cushioned chair in front of a mirror in a corner of the room and placed a small velvet chest full of jeweled hairpins and combs on a table beside the mirror. Mackenzie took her seat as soon as she was dressed. She watched her reflection self-consciously as the faery came up behind her with a brush in her hand.

"Your hair is your best feature," Nuala said as she began brushing. "It's like spun gold."

Mackenzie blushed. "I hate it. It's too thick. It never does what I want it to do."

"How can you hate it? It's luxurious, like silk." The faery wound a lock of Mackenzie's hair around her fingers and pinned it to the back of Mackenzie's head. "You're very pretty for a human girl. Your sister too, of course. It's too bad she's a cripple."

Mackenzie flinched at the cruel word. "Breanne's not crippled. She just limps a little bit."

The faery's silver eyes seemed to flicker as she stared at Mackenzie in the mirror. She pinned a second curl beside the first one. "I get the feeling you defend your sister a lot. Is she as loyal to you?"

"Breanne—has a chip on her shoulder sometimes," Mackenzie said with a nervous shrug. "She's still my sister."

❧

"Where were you?" Mackenzie mouthed as she and Breanne trailed behind Nuala several hours later.

Breanne shook her head, her lips compressed in a thin line. She'd been silent since being escorted back to the guest chamber. The stolen faery cloak had been taken from her. In its place she wore a white dress similar to the one Mackenzie was wearing. There'd been just enough time for one of the attendants to braid Breanne's hair and pin it up before Nuala returned from her own preparations to lead both sisters to the banquet.

"Are you okay?" Mackenzie whispered. "You look terrible. Your leg—it's dragging more than usual."

"And you look like you're wearing a wedding cake on your head," Breanne snapped.

Mackenzie lifted her hand to her hair. "I think the crystals look pretty."

"Whatever," said Breanne.

They turned one corner and then another until they reached the crowded hallway that led to the courtyard above ground. Without warning, Breanne grabbed Mackenzie's arm and yanked her backward.

"Hey—what are you doing?" said Mackenzie.

"Quickly," Breanne hissed in her ear. "Come on!"

The back of Nuala's head disappeared in the throng as Breanne dragged Mackenzie in the opposite direction.

"What are you doing?" Mackenzie repeated as Breanne pulled her into a dark alcove.

Breanne was breathing heavily. "We've got to find our way out of here. This is our chance!"

"What are you talking about?" Mackenzie said as she pulled her arm free. "I thought you liked it here."

"I don't like being trapped," Breanne said, peering around the edge of the alcove. "I spent hours walking in circles. I wanted to find the people we saw last night, but I couldn't get anywhere, no matter which way I went. Every time I turned a corner, I came to a dead end. There was no way out."

"Of course there's a way out," said Mackenzie. "We're on our way out right now."

"Listen to me—I couldn't get this far earlier," Breanne insisted. "Where we turned the corner just now, behind Nuala? It was a solid wall."

"What? What's wrong?" Breanne asked as she caught the expression on Mackenzie's face.

Mackenzie couldn't answer. She was transfixed by a pair of glowing eyes just even with Breanne's shoulder. She shrank back as a leathery creature with dark cavities where its nose should have been emerged from the shadows. The creature crept closer, hissing and licking its lips with a pointed tongue. It came so close she could smell its breath, like a dead animal after a day in the sun.

Breanne joined Mackenzie against the wall. "Oh God," Mackenzie said, grabbing her sister's arm and shutting her eyes.

She was praying for a quick and painless death when she heard an explosion of sharp clicks and hisses nearby.

"That's right, they're under protection," said a familiar voice. "Off with you."

Mackenzie opened her eyes in time to see the hunchbacked piper shooing the ugly creature away. The creature wasn't happy. It gnashed its teeth angrily as it edged slowly backward.

"Go on, quickly," said the piper. "Unless you want me to tell our friend Nuala that I found you salivating over her guests."

"Thank you," Mackenzie whispered. She was still clinging to her sister's sleeve. "Thank you, thank you, thank you."

The piper acknowledged them with a curt nod, his arms crossed. "Lucky for you I was in the neighborhood, wasn't it? That Pooka would have made a meal of you in no time, and he's not the worst thing about.

What possessed you to wander off by yourselves?"

Breanne didn't say anything. Mackenzie could feel her sister's anger radiating from her in waves.

The piper's eyes narrowed. "You've given your mistress the slip, haven't you?"

"What's it to you?" said Breanne.

"Breanne!" said Mackenzie. "Maybe he can help us."

The piper snorted. "Nay—I couldn't, even if I wanted to. Finian the piper has been seen with you now, hasn't he? Of all the faeries in the world below, you've managed to fall in with one of the most dangerous. Nuala is not the forgiving type. If you disappeared now, she'd have me roasted and fed to the wee creature I just chased away."

"What are you doing?" Breanne demanded as Finian took hold of each sister by the arm.

"The only thing I can do in the circumstances. I'm escorting you to the banquet."

"No way," Breanne said as she tried to wriggle free.

The piper tightened his grip. He was a strong man, in spite of his deformity. "Shhh. Haven't you already drawn enough attention to yourselves?"

Mackenzie felt a small package being thrust into her hand.

"Bogberries," Finian explained tersely. "Eat a handful before I start playing tonight. They're as sour as anything this side of the grave, but they'll help keep your mind from traveling too far."

"You knocked over that stool deliberately last night, didn't you?" Mackenzie whispered.

The piper didn't answer. "Come along," he said, urging them forward. "Quickly, before your mistress works herself into a temper."

CHAPTER SEVEN

N uala's eyes were the color of angry seas when they caught up with her by the giant doorway. She acknowledged the piper with the briefest of nods, then turned her back on him.

"Where did you disappear to?" she demanded peevishly, her hands on her hips. "I told the two of you to stay close!"

She didn't wait for a response but took the sisters by their wrists and hurried them across the courtyard. She had their seats rearranged so that they were on either side of her.

Mackenzie accepted small amounts of everything that was offered to her over the course of the evening, conscious of the faery's watchful eyes. She picked at the food without pleasure. Most of it remained on her plate.

"No appetite tonight?" Nuala asked as the dishes from the final course were cleared away. "You barely ate anything, either of you."

"What do you care what we eat?" Breanne asked sullenly. "Unless you're trying to fatten us up."

Mackenzie stopped breathing, her eyes fixed on the tablecloth in front of her.

"You're in a strange mood," the faery said coolly. "Did something happen to you when you wandered off?"

Out of the corner of her eye, Mackenzie saw her sister shrug.

"Hmm," said Nuala. "Perhaps a little music will improve your disposition."

Mackenzie's heart was already beating fast, but it sped up even more at the sight of the piper moving toward the center of the courtyard. The package of bogberries he'd given her was still concealed under a fold of fabric in her lap. With the faery sitting between her and Breanne all through dinner, she'd been unable to get any of the berries to her sister. She fingered the package anxiously as Finian sat down on his stool and prepared to play.

She acted on impulse, pouring a few berries into her palm and leaning forward as if to grab hold of her cup. She knocked it over instead. Nuala hissed as the crimson liquid streamed toward her.

"Oh, I'm so sorry!" Mackenzie cried as the faery pushed away from the table. "I'm so clumsy!" Mackenzie leaned across with a napkin in her hand as if she was going to wipe up the spilled drink. Instead she pretended to stumble, and her hand landed in her sister's lap. She released the berries she'd been clutching into her sister's palm. "Eat them, please!" she whispered.

"Why should I?" Breanne whispered back.

"We have to trust someone," Mackenzie said under her breath.

Two servants had stepped forward to clear the mess. "I'm so sorry," Mackenzie repeated as Nuala dabbed at a stain on her dress. While everyone was still distracted, Mackenzie slipped a few bogberries into her own mouth.

She felt her entire face pucker as the berry skins dissolved on her tongue. With an effort, Mackenzie managed to swallow the fruit, but the sourness in her mouth was still overpowering. Immediately the sounds around her were muffled, as if the effect of the berries had overflowed into her eardrums as well. She was only vaguely aware that the piper had begun to play. It was like being under water and far away from everyone else. The pipe music was haunting, but it didn't take hold of her the way it had the night before. She could still think. She was still conscious of where she was.

Mackenzie glanced at her sister out of the corner of her eye. It was impossible to tell if Breanne had eaten her berries too.

The music went on and on. Mackenzie lost track of time. Eventually the tiny lights that hovered over the courtyard faded and went out. In the torchlight that remained, Mackenzie watched a procession of faeries in scarlet cloaks approach from the other side of the courtyard. The first faery carried the two-handled cup that she remembered from the night before. He led the procession to a flat stone a few yards away from the piper and set the cup down. Then he joined the others in a circle around the stone.

Finian was still playing. Mackenzie could just hear his music spiraling up into the night. There was a flicker above her head, and a sheet of pale green fire ignited across the sky. The cold flames grew brighter as the piper held one long note. Without warning, the sky exploded in a flash of blinding light.

Several seconds passed before Mackenzie was willing to open her eyes again. The music had stopped. The sky was dark, and everything around her was in shadow. A faint light came from the surface of the solstice cup, which was now in the hands of a tall faery at a nearby table. Mackenzie watched help-lessly as the faery presented the cup to a young girl dressed in white. Without hesitating, the girl raised the cup to her lips. Mackenzie held her breath as the girl drank. A tremor passed through the girl's body, and then she was still again.

The solstice cup was offered to two more girls and a boy before it reached Mackenzie's table. She glanced anxiously at Breanne while Nuala's attention was diverted. "Pretend," her sister mouthed. Mackenzie nodded, feeling a wave of relief that her sister was still alert.

Nuala presented the cup to Breanne first this time. Breanne lifted the cup to her mouth, but it was impossible to tell if any of the pale liquid passed through her lips. The silver-eyed faery took the cup back and turned to Mackenzie. Mackenzie accepted the cup with shaking hands, conscious that she was being watched. Somehow she managed to get it up to her lips without spilling anything. She tilted the cup and then brought it down quickly before any liquid could reach her mouth.

When she had the cup back again, Nuala raised a jeweled finger. Instantly two attendants stepped forward to escort the sisters back to their chamber.

❧

"Tell me you didn't drink any of that stuff," Mackenzie demanded the second she and Breanne were alone in their room.

Breanne unfastened her white gown. "It wasn't that bad. Kind of bland, like sugar water."

"Breanne!" Mackenzie raised her hands to her mouth. "How could you?"

"Oh, stop freaking. Of course I didn't. I'm not an idiot."

Mackenzie grabbed a cushion from the nearest chair and threw it at her sister. "You're going to give me a heart attack one day, you know that?"

❧

Breanne was not in the canopy bed when Mackenzie woke up the next morning. She wasn't anywhere in the room. Mackenzie threw aside the covers and hurried to the doorway. She drew back instantly at the sound of tiny bells coming down the corridor. When Nuala and one of her attendants entered the room, Mackenzie was sitting nervously on the unmade bed.

"You're up," said the faery. She sounded surprised. "Where's your sister this time?" she asked, glancing quickly around the room.

Mackenzie bit her lip. "I-I'm not sure."

Nuala's eyes darkened instantly. She said something sharp in her own language to the attendant beside her, and the girl curtsied and backed out of the room.

The faery took a deep breath and shifted her attention to Mackenzie again. "Your sister is a hard one to keep track of, isn't she?" she asked as her eyes returned to their usual color. "It's too bad she's not here. I wanted to show you both something this morning. But I can still show you, can't I?"

Mackenzie tensed as the faery came across the room and sat down beside her, taking her hand. "I-I think I should wait for Breanne. In case something's happened to her..."

Nuala sighed impatiently. "You really have to stop worrying about your sister. She doesn't worry about you, does she? She ran off without you. She didn't even tell you where she was going this time."

Mackenzie didn't meet the faery's eyes.

"Oh, come on," said Nuala. "Don't let her spoil everything for you. Get dressed—we'll only be gone for a few hours."

Mackenzie's hand began to burn under the faery's fingers. "I guess I could go—if we're only going to be gone for a little while."

For the third time in as many days, Mackenzie followed Nuala along the route that led outside to the courtyard. They passed a few other faeries and a number of hooded servants on their way, but the courtyard itself was vacant. In the gray light of morning, it looked abandoned. Where there had been tables and chairs just a few hours before, there were only crumbling boulders scattered across a mossy stone floor.

Mackenzie turned to Nuala, her eyes wide.

The faery waved her hand, dismissing the scene in front of them. "This isn't what I brought you to see. Come, over here."

She took Mackenzie's elbow and steered her toward a flat boulder at the center of the courtyard. It was the only thing Mackenzie recognized from the banquet the night before: the flat stone that had held the solstice cup. Mackenzie hesitated at the sight of a shallow depression on top of the waist-high stone. It was filled with a pearly white liquid.

Nuala pulled her forward. "You're not afraid, are you?" she asked slyly. "After all, you drank from this pool last night."

Mackenzie's face flamed. "I-I—"

"Don't worry," the faery laughed. "I'm not going to force you to drink anything. Even though I know you were faking it last night, you naughty girl! Calm down," she said when Mackenzie began to tremble. "I'm not going to hurt you. I just wanted to show you something."

Nuala reached across the stone and stirred the small pool with her finger. "Solstice fire has many properties: light in the winter sky, liquid when we call it down. And it can reveal things. Are you curious?"

The shimmering liquid had become more transparent as the faery stirred it, until it was almost like water. "I guess so," Mackenzie said uncertainly.

"Then look closely," Nuala said as she withdrew her hand. "Do you see anyone you recognize?"

Mackenzie bent over the stone. A scene flickered into focus just beneath the surface of the small pool. Two pale shapes moved against a dark background. As she watched, the shapes resolved themselves into girls, and then the girls into younger versions of Mackenzie and Breanne.

"That's me, that's us," Mackenzie said, looking up at Nuala in surprise. She looked down again quickly. "I think—I think that's the night..." Her voice dropped away.

"It seems you've been at the threshold of our world once before," said the faery.

Mackenzie watched the two small girls climb the hill behind their aunt and uncle's farmhouse. It was as if someone had taken her memory of that evening five years before and projected it into the pool. The young Breanne was first up to the three ancient stones that formed a child-sized arch against the sky. She was always first back then, before her leg was injured. The young Mackenzie caught up with her sister a few seconds later. Breanne tagged her, and the two girls chased each other around the squat stones, first one way and then the other.

The sun was low in the sky as they finished their game and collapsed in the grass. Breanne turned her head toward the stones and scrambled suddenly to her feet. She'd seen something in the shadows, something that made her crouch next to the stones.

When she stood up again, her fingers were curled around something shiny.

The young Mackenzie wanted to see the treasure Breanne had found, but Breanne turned away. Mackenzie pleaded and craned her neck to see over her sister's shoulder. Finally Breanne turned. There on her outstretched palm was a gold ring with a large purple stone. It was beautiful, more beautiful than anything Mackenzie had ever seen in their mother's jewelry box. She reached out to touch it, but Breanne drew her hand back quickly.

Then the young Mackenzie saw something move behind her sister in the shadow of the stones. It was an arm, long and thin, reaching out from the dark space beneath the arch. Mackenzie froze as a hand began to move over the ground at the base of the stones. Three long bony fingers and a thumb, patting the ground, feeling for something. The older Mackenzie, the one watching the scene from above, knew instantly what the hand was searching for. The younger Mackenzie did too. She sprang to life, lunging for the ring in her sister's hand. She wrestled it free and flung it into the shadows. Before her sister could react, the young Mackenzie grabbed Breanne's arm and dragged her down the hill.

Breanne fought back. They'd traveled just a few yards before she managed to wrench her arm free. The younger Mackenzie's attention was focused entirely on her sister. In her desperation to pull Breanne to safety, she didn't see the hideous creature crouched beneath the arch. The older Mackenzie saw it. She saw the Pooka raise a hollow bone to its lips. It puffed its leathery cheeks, and a tiny dart flew from the end of the bone. Breanne yelped and collapsed, clutching her ankle.

"I thought she'd stumbled, that she'd twisted her ankle as I was trying to get her down the hill," the older Mackenzie whispered, her eyes still fixed on the scene reflected in the pool. "But then it never got better. We were best friends before that, but then—"

"All this time your sister has blamed you for her leg," Nuala said. "But the truth is, you saved her. Look."

Mackenzie watched her sister rock back and forth in pain. She watched the younger version of herself yank Breanne to her feet and half drag, half carry the moaning girl down the hill. The shadow cast by the stones behind them had gotten longer as the sun descended. The Pooka crept forward to the edge of the shadow and then stopped, as if it had reached an invisible barrier.

"You were lucky you got your sister away before the sun set," said Nuala. "A few more minutes and that Pooka could have roamed anywhere in the dark."

The pool turned opaque again. Mackenzie looked up.

"You poor thing," Nuala said, patting Mackenzie's hand. "She hasn't been very grateful, has she? But I know you still love her," she said with a resigned sigh, "which is why I have one more thing to show you."

The faery reached into the folds of her skirt and withdrew a tiny brown bird. One of the bird's wings was broken, its feathers twisted and bloody.

"I know how cautious you are," the faery said as she stroked the trembling bird. "I admire that, really. Human girls are usually so impulsive, like your sister. They never stop to think about the consequences of anything they do. But you're different, aren't you? For example, I couldn't just tell you that solstice fire has healing properties. You'd need to see it for yourself."

"What do you mean?" Mackenzie asked.

"Listen," said Nuala. "I know you were only trying to protect your sister when you knocked the cup from her hand two nights ago, and when you convinced her not to drink last night. But one sip and her leg would be right again. Don't you want that for her?"

Mackenzie stared at the bird, too nervous to meet the faery's eyes.

"Watch," said Nuala patiently. She lifted the bird above the white pool. "See how its wing is broken?" The bird struggled as Nuala lowered it slowly into the opaque liquid. "Now look!"

The transformation was immediate. The bird shuddered, and its twisted feathers settled neatly into place. It spread its wings and tucked them in again by its side. The blood had vanished. Both wings were straight and undamaged.

The faery raised her hand, and the bird flew to her fingers. "There—you've seen for yourself what the solstice fire can do," she said as she stroked the bird's feathers. "Any questions?"

Mackenzie shook her head. "I-I don't think so."

"I knew you'd understand," Nuala said, her eyes gleaming. "Now we just have to convince your sister."

CHAPTER EIGHT

Breanne was sitting cross-legged on the bed when Nuala brought Mackenzie back from the courtyard.

"I have to leave you for a while," Nuala said from the doorway. "I'll have some food sent in while I'm gone. Eat up while you can—there's no banquet tonight. Tonight we ride."

"What is that supposed to mean, 'Tonight we ride'?" Breanne asked after Nuala was gone. "And where were you?"

"Where were *you*?" said Mackenzie.

"Looking for a way out of here. Where did you think I was?" Breanne punched the pillow in her lap. "She's delusional if she thinks she can keep me in here forever."

"We need to talk," Mackenzie said.

"I'm serious, I'm not going to be anyone's prisoner."

Mackenzie yanked her sister's pillow away. "Listen to me, Breanne!"

"What?" Breanne asked angrily.

Mackenzie took a breath. "I would never leave you behind," she said through gritted teeth. "But you keep taking off on me, your sister, your *twin* sister."

Breanne shrugged. "I don't know what you're getting so excited about. You were asleep. Besides, you're too chicken to go anywhere anyway."

"What I'm getting excited about?" Mackenzie threw up her hands angrily. "Sisters are supposed to stick together, Breanne! That's why I'm here in the first place, because I came with you! Because I wouldn't let you go off by yourself and get lost!"

"So you shouldn't have followed me then," Breanne said with contempt. "Your mistake."

"My *mistake*? I fell into a river trying to save your *life*, Breanne! And it's not the first time."

"Not the first time that you fell into a river?"

"That I saved your life, you moron!" Mackenzie stomped across the room and sat down hard on the canopy bed. "Remember that night at the stones five years ago? There *was* something there—a Pooka! It shot you with a dart, in the ankle. If I hadn't been there to drag you down the hill, it would have caught you for sure!"

"I was there," said Breanne. "There was no *Pooka*. You're the one who wrecked my ankle when you yanked me so hard!"

"That's not what happened," said Mackenzie. "Nuala showed me, in the pool."

Breanne snorted. "What pool?"

"A pool of solstice fire—the stuff from the solstice cup. I saw everything that happened that night."

"Oh, really?" Breanne said sarcastically.

"Yes, really! It was like watching a movie. Plus the solstice fire has healing properties. Nuala said if you drank it, your leg would be back to normal."

Breanne's eyebrows disappeared under her bangs. "Are you kidding me? Last night we couldn't drink from the solstice cup because the piper guy said we'd turn into zombie slaves. Now Nuala says 'drink up,' and suddenly you want to do what *she* says. Which is it, Mackenzie? Too bad we can't call Mom and ask her opinion, since you can't seem to think for yourself."

"That's not fair," Mackenzie said angrily. "I *saw* the bird get healed! It had a broken wing, and Nuala put it in the pool and the wing was fixed, just like that. There was no more blood or anything!"

"Just like that," Breanne repeated in a mocking voice. "So what are you saying? You think we should drink a little 'solstice fire' after all?"

Mackenzie crossed her arms. "I don't *know*! I'm just telling you what I saw. I was trying to help you!"

They were interrupted by the sound of footsteps outside the room. One of Nuala's attendants entered the doorway with a large platter of food.

Breanne got up from the bed. "Maybe you can settle this for us," she said as the attendant set the tray down on a table. "What do you think, should we drink from the magic cup or not? My sister can't seem to make up her mind."

The servant didn't even pause. Her expression remained blank as she turned to exit the room.

"Hello, anyone in there?" Breanne asked, waving her hand in front of the girl's face.

"Breanne, stop it!" said Mackenzie.

Breanne moved her body to block the doorway. "I just want an answer."

"She *can't* answer you," said Mackenzie. "Breanne, you're scaring her! Let her go!"

"It's a simple question," said Breanne. "Did you drink from the solstice cup? Is that why you're the way you are?"

The attendant looked at her feet.

"Just shake your head, yes or no," Breanne said impatiently.

There was still no response. "Come on, answer me!" Breanne said, taking hold of the girl's shoulders and shaking her. The hood slipped back from the girl's red hair.

Mackenzie was across the room in an instant. "What's wrong with you?" she said as she yanked her sister away.

"Stay out of my way!" Breanne shouted. She wrenched her arm free and slapped Mackenzie in the face. Mackenzie held her cheek, too stunned to speak.

"I was *trying* to get some information," Breanne said when the attendant had fled. "How else are we supposed to know who to trust in this place?"

"Who to trust? Who to *trust*?" said Mackenzie. "The one person I should be able to count on is my own sister. But look at you, Breanne! You've totally lost it!"

"Just leave me alone," Breanne said. She stomped back to the bed and turned to face the wall.

Mackenzie tried to sleep in a chair while she waited for Nuala's return, but she was too upset. The hours passed slowly as she and Breanne did their best to ignore each other. Mackenzie was almost relieved when she finally heard the tinkling sound of Nuala's belled slippers approaching in the corridor.

"Here comes our evil faery godmother," Breanne said as she threw her legs over the side of the bed. "Quick, give me some of those berries."

"I don't think so," Mackenzie said from her seat in the opposite corner of the room.

"What do you mean, 'I don't think so'?"

"You owe me an apology first," Mackenzie said as she stood up. "For once, I'm going to hear you say you're sorry."

Breanne's eyes went to the doorway. "We don't have time for this, Mackenzie. Come on, give me those berries."

Mackenzie shrugged. "Maybe I don't have any left."

"Don't be stupid," Breanne hissed. "Just give me some of the freakin' berries, before it's too late!"

Mackenzie's heart was racing, but she shook her head. "Not until you apologize."

Nuala and two of her attendants appeared in the doorway before Breanne could say anything more.

"You're both still here—wonderful," said the faery. She signaled her servants to step forward with two heavy cloaks in their arms. Mackenzie ignored her sister's scathing expression as she accepted one of the cloaks and put it on.

"Is something wrong?" said Nuala, looking pointedly at Breanne.

Breanne had taken her cloak from the second gray-hooded girl and draped it over the back of the nearest chair. "I don't really feel like going out this evening. But thanks for the invitation anyway."

Nuala's eyes narrowed. She said something in her own language, and the nearest attendant picked up the cloak and handed it to the faery. "I'm afraid staying behind isn't an option," Nuala said calmly as she arranged the cloak around Breanne's shoulders. "Everyone rides on the third night of the solstice festival. It's just the way it is."

Mackenzie saw Breanne stiffen as if she'd received a shock when the faery fastened the clasp at her neck. Mackenzie bit her lip and looked away.

The closer they got to the courtyard, the guiltier Mackenzie felt for withholding the bogberries from Breanne. She fingered the pouch under her cloak as she hurried down the crowded corridor. She had counted the shriveled berries it contained that morning. There were thirty berries, enough for her and Breanne to have three berries each for the remaining nights of the winter festival. But Breanne was out of reach on the other side of Nuala, and the faery had them both firmly by the arms.

Mackenzie heard the pipes playing before they'd even reached the giant doorway to the courtyard. Her stomach did a somersault. "I'm sorry!" she mouthed to Breanne as they were swept through the portal in a crush of excited faeries.

Breanne didn't blink. Her eyes were ice chips, her face a blank mask. "I hate you," she mouthed back.

Something snapped inside Mackenzie. "Fine, be like that," she whispered angrily, her fingers already scrabbling inside the pouch. She checked that no one was watching and slipped half a dozen berries into her mouth. Her eyes welled up instantly. She had to force herself to swallow the sour fruit.

She forgot about her taste buds and everything else when she saw the courtyard. It was packed with the strangest beasts she'd ever seen. Foxes with hooves skittered between the legs of gigantic centipedes. Goats with iridescent wings pawed the air. A terrifying animal with the body of a horse and the head of an eagle rose up on its hind legs as a faery leaped onto its back. There were ponies with scales and lizards with feathers, giant bug-eyed grasshoppers and moths with wings the size of sails.

"Do you see any you like?" Mackenzie heard Nuala shout as an enormous eel with three riders came thrashing past.

Mackenzie was speechless. Even Breanne looked dumbfounded.

Nuala tilted her head back and let out a wild laugh. "It's my favorite night of the year!" She tightened her grip on the girls' arms. "Come on, we'll find something gentler for you to ride."

"Something gentler" was a shaggy pony with dragonfly wings for Mackenzie, and a white, otter-like creature the same size as the pony for Breanne.

"Climb up, quickly," Nuala hissed in Mackenzie's ear. "You'll be trampled if you're still on the ground when the first mount takes off."

Mackenzie's pony made a faint nickering sound as she grabbed hold of the base of its mane and pulled herself up. Getting around the wings was difficult, but the pony cooperated by standing still. Mackenzie found the securest position she could, pressing her legs against the pony's forelegs and wrapping her arms tightly around the pony's neck.

Breanne was already mounted when Mackenzie looked up. The otter-creature seemed to be trying to shake her sister off, but Breanne's arms and legs were wound tightly around the otter's body. Her mouth was set in a determined line.

Nuala appeared an instant later on a silver mount with the head and forelegs of a horse and the tail and hind legs of a giant lizard. "Hold tight!" Mackenzie heard her shout. "We're about to ride!"

Mackenzie became aware of the pipes again for the first time since swallowing the bogberries. The muffled notes rose above the din around them. Mackenzie's pony pawed the ground, anxious to be off. Mackenzie felt her own muscles tense as the piper played a single, sustained note that made everything seem to vibrate.

A great *crack* split the sky with the force of a thousand whips. Mackenzie tightened her limbs and grabbed fistfuls of shaggy fur as the pony hurtled forward. The ground was a blur beneath them, and then it was nothing at all as the pony took off into the air. They joined the other mounted beasts, a train of leaping, thrashing shadows climbing into the night. Mackenzie buried her head in the pony's mane, clinging blindly to its back. A voice cried out somewhere ahead of them, and the pony wheeled sharply to the left. The voice cried again, and the pony wheeled to the right. Mackenzie tasted the berries she'd eaten rising in her throat. She had to fight not to throw them up.

Time lost its meaning as the wild ride stretched on through the night. The piper's music traveled with them, sometimes calling the riders from ahead, sometimes goading them from behind. Mackenzie's muscles burned with the effort of staying on her mount. The music was like a distant soundtrack of her agony.

"Please," she prayed desperately, her eyes shut tight, "help me hold on—help us both hold on until we get wherever we're going."

The ride went on and on. Mackenzie had almost given up hope that it would ever end when she felt her mount descend sharply. There was a shock of impact as the pony's hooves met something solid. She opened her eyes a crack. The sky was alight with sheets of pale green flame stretching in every direction. Beneath the sky, the pony galloped across an uneven landscape of rocks and brambles.

The pipes grew louder. Mackenzie wasn't sure if they were getting closer, or if the effect of the bogberries was wearing off. The beasts in the wild ride slowed and came to an uneasy stop back in the courtyard where they'd begun. Mackenzie heard a single note rise above the others, and the sky grew even brighter. She covered her face just before the sky exploded.

She didn't open her eyes again until she felt a hand touch her thigh. She expected Nuala, but it was one of the faery's attendants instead. With the girl's help, Mackenzie dismounted. Her breath was ragged. Standing upright was painful, even with the servant's arm supporting her. "Where's my sister? Where's Breanne?" she croaked.

Mackenzie searched the attendant's face, but it was vacant as always. "Please," she begged, her heart pounding. "Take me to Nuala!"

The girl led her through a tangle of pawing, snorting beasts. The sky was dark again. By torchlight, Mackenzie saw a ring of faeries gathered around the flat stone at the center of the courtyard. There were two figures inside the circle. The taller figure held a two-handled cup, brimming with a luminescent liquid. She passed it to the figure in white.

"Stop!" Mackenzie cried.

She was too far away. Breanne was already lifting the cup to her lips.

"No!" Mackenzie shouted as she forced her way through the circle of faeries.

Nuala had already taken the cup back when Mackenzie reached her sister's side. "Please, Breanne," Mackenzie begged. "Tell me you didn't do it. Tell me you didn't really drink anything!"

"It's done," Nuala said, her eyes shining. "Why are you so upset? The solstice fire healed your sister's leg, as I said it would."

Mackenzie grabbed her sister's hands, ignoring the faery. "Are you all right? Breanne—look at me. Breanne!"

Breanne turned. There was no recognition in her eyes.

CHAPTER NINE

Two gray-hooded attendants escorted Mackenzie and Breanne back to their chamber. Mackenzie couldn't tell whether her sister was limping or not. Breanne's limbs were like spaghetti. The attendant helping Breanne almost had to carry her at times. When they reached their room, Breanne's escort helped her out of her gown and into the canopy bed. Breanne began to snore softly the instant her head hit the pillow.

Mackenzie slipped under the covers beside her sister as soon as the attendants were gone. Every muscle in her body ached from the faery ride, but she was wide awake. She stared at the silk canopy above her head for the remainder of the night, listening anxiously to each breath that entered and left her sister's body.

In the early hours of the morning, Breanne began to give off an alarming amount of heat. Mackenzie felt her sister's forehead and withdrew her fingers quickly, as if she'd touched a hot iron.

"Breanne!" Mackenzie whispered urgently. "Breanne, you're burning up—you have to wake up!"

Breanne didn't stir.

Mackenzie yanked off all the covers and leaned over her sister. "Breanne, please—wake up!"

There was a candle near the bed. Mackenzie grabbed it and scoured the room. She found a pitcher of water and ran back to pour it over her sister's body.

Breanne's eyes fluttered open. "It's all falling apart," she mumbled. "You can see it if you look sideways. Everything's crumbling."

"What did you say?" Mackenzie grabbed her sister's hand. "Breanne, you're not making any sense."

"I'm so tired," said Breanne. "Let me sleep."

❧

Mackenzie was still clutching Breanne's hand when Nuala appeared in the doorway later in the morning. Mackenzie jumped to her feet.

"What's wrong with my sister?" she demanded in a strained voice. "She's on fire! I can't get her to drink anything—I can't even get her to wake up! What did that stuff do to her?"

"You need to be patient," Nuala said calmly as she came toward the bed. "Of course she's tired. That just shows the solstice fire is working. She'll be awake again in a few days, rested and renewed."

"In a few days? But you said she was healed last night."

"I said her *leg* was healed last night," the faery corrected. She leaned over and brushed Breanne's forearm with her fingertips. "Be honest—there are other things about your sister that need adjusting. How stubborn she is, for example. Her nasty temper."

Mackenzie shook her head. "You didn't say you were going to change her."

Nuala sighed as she turned to Mackenzie. "It's sweet how much you care about your sister. Really it is. But you need to look after yourself. Look at you. You've got huge circles under your eyes. You're shaking. You look awful."

Mackenzie held her breath as the faery took both of her hands.

"Listen—if you're so worried about your sister, why don't you join her? Then you'll see for yourself how safe she is."

"You mean drink from the solstice cup," said Mackenzie.

"There's nothing to be afraid of," Nuala said with a hint of impatience. "I'll drink from the cup myself tonight if that's what it takes to convince you."

She stood up, still holding one of Mackenzie's hands. "In the meantime, I'm taking you outside. We're joining the party."

"I-I can't leave Breanne like this," said Mackenzie. She braced herself, half expecting to be stung for her refusal.

"You have a bit of a stubborn streak yourself, don't you?" said Nuala, her silver eyes unblinking. "Fine," she sighed. "Stay with your sister for now. But you still have to come to the banquet tonight."

Mackenzie tried to rouse her sister again as soon as the faery was gone. Breanne's lips twitched when Mackenzie shook her shoulder, but her eyes remained closed.

"What have I done, what have I done?" said Mackenzie as she paced the room, clenching and unclenching her hands.

"You've let your sister bond herself to Nuala—that's what you've done," said a voice behind her. Mackenzie spun around to find the hunchbacked piper standing in the doorway. "Seven years of service for that wee sip."

Mackenzie's voice broke. "You have to help me. I don't know what to do!"

Finian entered the room and crossed over to the bed. "Seems it's your sister that needs help now."

"Please," said Mackenzie. "I didn't mean for anything to happen to her. Nuala said the solstice fire would heal her leg. She showed me: the bird's wing was broken and then it was fixed."

The piper snorted. "Heal her leg, is that what she said? Her limp will be gone, aye, along with her memory, her will and everything else that makes her herself. The fire burns it all away. She'll be just like the rest of them for the next seven years."

"The rest of them?"

"The gray-hoods, the other lads and lasses lured down below," Finian said impatiently. He settled his misshapen frame in the chair closest to the bed and leaned forward. "I warned you, you can't say I didn't. There are a handful of selfish faeries like Nuala who entice young humans down below every solstice to serve them. Nuala herself has built up quite a collection."

"No." Mackenzie shook her head. "There has to be a way to get Breanne out of this."

"Come back in seven years," said the piper. "She'll be free as a bird then."

"I can't leave my sister here for seven years!"

"Not much choice. Leave her here, or drink from the cup and join her."

Tears had begun to leak down Mackenzie's face. She crouched beside the bed and took her sister's burning hand. "Please," she begged, still looking at Finian. "This is my fault. If I'd given her the berries when she asked for them, she wouldn't be like this. I'll do whatever it takes. I have to save her!"

"Whatever it takes?" Finian shrugged. "Easy to say now."

Mackenzie wiped her cheeks angrily. "I mean it! Whatever I have to do, I'll do it."

"Mmm," said the piper, one eyebrow raised. "'Tis a shame the pair of you didn't stay put with the old woman in the first place." He caught the surprise on Mackenzie's face and nodded. "Aye, I know Maigret. And I know the distress you caused her when you left so ungratefully. Believe me, I wouldn't be here if she hadn't asked me to look out for you. I'm risking my neck just being in this room," he said, rising to his feet.

Mackenzie stood up quickly. "Can Maigret help us? Will you take me to her?"

"Not at this hour," said Finian as he moved toward the door. "I'll be back for you tonight, after the banquet, when it's safer."

"Promise?" Mackenzie said anxiously.

There was no mirth in the piper's laugh. "Promises are tin coins in this world, lassie. But I'll be here."

❧

Mackenzie was the only human guest at the banquet that night. The faeries around her ate and drank with abandon. Their laughter seemed shriller and their arguments more intense than at the previous two feasts Mackenzie had attended. She kept her head down, trying not to draw attention to herself. She was relieved when Finian appeared at the center of the courtyard with his pipes. When no one was watching, she slipped a few bogberries into her mouth.

Everything after that was as it had been at the last banquet. Finian's music was muffled thanks to the sour berries, but Mackenzie could still hear it rising up into the night sky. The sky responded with the same spectacular display. Sheets of pale flame illuminated a procession of scarlet-robed faeries bearing the solstice cup to the flat stone in the center of the courtyard. Mackenzie was ready for the brilliant explosion this time.

When she opened her eyes again, Nuala was gliding toward her with the cup in her hands. Mackenzie held her breath as the faery stopped and raised the cup to her own mouth.

"See?" Nuala said softly when she'd lowered the cup again. Her lips were wet and they glowed faintly. "I told you it was safe. Now it's your turn." She held the cup out for Mackenzie.

Mackenzie couldn't meet the faery's eyes. Her hands remained at her sides. "I still can't," she whispered.

Nuala let out an angry hiss. "That's four times you've refused this cup. Why do you resist? *How* do you resist?"

Mackenzie didn't say anything. She swallowed, but the lump in her throat remained.

"It's very curious," said the faery. She stared at Mackenzie for a long moment and then raised her fingers. One of her attendants stepped forward from the shadows to escort Mackenzie back underground.

CHAPTER TEN

Mackenzie had almost worn a path in the rugs underfoot before Finian finally showed up at the door of her chamber. "I was afraid you weren't coming," she said, releasing her breath gratefully.

"I'm here," said the piper. "Let's go. Quickly. Follow a few paces behind, and don't speak."

Mackenzie took her sister's hand before leaving the room. Breanne's skin was still warm, but nowhere near the temperature it had been. Finian was already halfway down the corridor when Mackenzie slipped through the door after him.

The piper moved swiftly, turning one way and then the other without hesitation. They were traveling in the opposite direction to the route that led up to the courtyard. Finian stopped abruptly at one corner and motioned with his hand for Mackenzie to stay back. Mackenzie held her breath, her heart hammering in her chest, until Finian signaled that it was safe again. A few minutes later, Mackenzie followed the piper up a set of shallow stairs. She could smell the tang of marsh air as she climbed the last few steps. Then they were outside.

"Can you see well enough to walk?" the piper said softly. He had stopped to let Mackenzie catch up.

"I think so," Mackenzie whispered. There were no torches to illuminate their path, and the stars were hidden behind clouds. But there was a faint smudge of light all around the lower edge of the sky. "Is it safe to talk now?"

"Not if you value your pretty skin," said Finian. "You never know what's lurking in the shadows."

As if to prove his point, small rustling noises accompanied them all the way down to the tree-lined avenues where Mackenzie had had her first glimpse of faery revelry. The avenues were deserted now. Finian led her across one road and down another, and then they descended a steep staircase to the stony beach.

"Do we have to wade across?" Mackenzie asked as her eyes found the silhouette of a small building on stilts a short distance offshore.

Finian snorted. "You can wade if you want to, lass. I'd prefer to row."

He motioned for Mackenzie to follow. A few yards farther down the shore, there was a narrow inlet that

Mackenzie hadn't noticed when she'd arrived on the island with Breanne. Half a dozen boats of various shapes and sizes were moored along a low wharf. Finian liberated a small wooden rowboat and steadied Mackenzie while she climbed in.

Mackenzie turned her head away as the piper began to pull the oars. His strokes might have looked awkward, but they were efficient. The crossing took only a few minutes. Mackenzie waited by the ladder that led up to Maigret's shack while Finian tied up the boat.

"Go on then," said the piper gruffly. "She won't bite. She'll be relieved to see that you're all right."

Halfway up the ladder, Mackenzie heard the trap-door above her head creak open an inch.

"Strange time to be visiting an old woman," came Maigret's voice. "Who is it, and what do you want?"

Mackenzie's grip tightened on the ladder rung. "It's me, Mackenzie—one of the girls you pulled out of the water a few days ago. Finian brought me back."

The trapdoor swung open all the way. "Well come up then! What are you waiting for?" said Maigret.

The interior of the shack was pitch black. Mackenzie felt callused hands take her wrists as she neared the top of the ladder. The old woman guided her through the opening in the floor and helped her to her feet.

"Are you still yourself then?" said Maigret. "What about your sister—where is she?"

"That's why I brought this one here," Mackenzie heard Finian say as he came up through the trapdoor behind her. "I warned them, I slipped them enough bogberries to last the week and then some. But the other one drank from the cup anyway."

Mackenzie felt Maigret's grip tighten as she said something in a language Mackenzie didn't understand. She sounded cross.

"Aye, I know what you asked me to do," said the piper. "I did my part."

"It was my fault," Mackenzie said quickly. "I had the berries. I was waiting for her to apologize. I mean—I didn't give them to my sister when she asked for them."

The old woman sighed heavily and released Mackenzie's arms. "Well. There's no use cursing the path that brought you here. What's done is done. Wait, I'll light a lamp."

Mackenzie heard Maigret move away. There was the sound of friction, as if two rocks were being rubbed together, and a tiny flame appeared inside a lamp on the other side of the room. The flame grew brighter as Maigret adjusted it. Mackenzie's eyes went instinctively to the window that faced the faery island, but it was shuttered, as was the one across from it.

"You can breathe easy, lass," Maigret said. "None of the fair folk has ever bothered me here. You're safe."

"But my sister—"

"Aye, your sister." Maigret frowned. "Now that's another matter."

"There must be something you can give her," Mackenzie said hopefully, eyeing the dried herbs that hung in bunches from the rafters in a corner of the room. "When Breanne was unconscious in the marsh, you woke her up with some kind of 'birthing' herb."

"Aye, I did."

"Well, can you wake her up now?" Mackenzie asked.

Maigret shook her head, her thin lips pursed. "There's naught I can give her for this. The solstice cup is too powerful—the bond too strong. That's why I tried to keep you here, out of harm's way."

Mackenzie looked down at the floorboards. "I'm sorry. I didn't want to go. I tried to talk her out of it…"

The old woman waved her hand. "'Tis over and done. You're here now, and you're after a way to save your sister."

"Yes," said Mackenzie.

"Come, sit down." Maigret motioned Mackenzie over to the pile of wool blankets in the corner of the room.

Mackenzie sat against the wall, her arms around her knees. The old woman remained standing a few feet away. Finian had already seated himself on the one stool in the room.

"There might be a way to free your sister," Maigret said after a moment of reflection. "The magic that holds your sister is very old and very powerful. Naught but the strongest bond could ever hope to stand against it. But you are twins, womb-sisters, and there is no stronger bond than that. It might be enough, if you have the will and the courage."

"Whatever I have to do, I'll do it," said Mackenzie.

Maigret nodded at the pile of baskets across the room. "I am tolerated in the world below because I make myself useful here. I catch eels and fish for the banquet tables. I gather eggs from the marsh nests in season." Her gaze moved to the crude wooden frame behind Finian, in the opposite corner. "I also weave on that loom when I am asked. There are others on the island who weave, some of the solstice-bound, but my silks are finer than anyone else's. The fair folk compete for my handiwork."

"You'd never know it by the rags Maigret wears herself, would you?" Finian said wryly, his arms crossed.

"I take nothing from the faerie, so they can take nothing from me," Maigret said calmly. "Finian knows that. The question is, can you use a loom, lass?"

"I've never tried."

The old woman clicked her tongue. "A pity, but I suppose I can teach you warp from weft. That won't be the worst of your challenges."

"I have to weave something to free my sister?" Mackenzie asked, trying to follow the conversation.

"Aye, a mantle to throw over her shoulders during the Sealing Ceremony, three nights hence. You'll need to weave it out of special fibers. I can gather grasses from the edges in the morning." Maigret squinted at Mackenzie's dress. "Do you still have the garments you were wearing when you arrived?"

"I think so," said Mackenzie. She blushed. "We hid them behind some rocks on the shore so we wouldn't have to come back here."

"Good. You'll need fibers from your sister's clothing to return her to herself, and fibers from your own garments to bind your sister to you until you're both safely away. There's one more thing..." The old woman peered at Mackenzie's anxious face and left her sentence unfinished. "But you have enough to think about for now. That will get you started."

She motioned for Mackenzie to stand up. "Best be on your way back to the island. You can tear a few pieces from your clothing when you reach the shore. Give them to Finian for safekeeping until he brings you back tomorrow night."

Mackenzie got up reluctantly. "Do I have to go back tonight? I can't stay here with you?"

"No, lass, you can't stay here." Maigret shook her head. "Nuala would turn the island upside down if you disappeared now. 'Twould only be a matter of time before someone came looking for you here. You must be in your room when she checks on you in the morning."

"All right." Mackenzie swallowed. "It's just that Nuala is still trying to make me take the solstice cup. It's hard to say no, and I think she suspects about the berries."

"Then you must pretend to drink from the cup the next time she offers it to you."

"But in the morning she'll know I faked it," said Mackenzie. "If she doesn't figure it out right away."

"I have a remedy for that," said the old woman. She was already across the room, rummaging in a basket. "Take a pinch of the herbs I'm about to give you, sprinkled in a cup of water, just before you go to sleep. You'll wake with a fever. Not high enough to do harm—just high enough to fool Nuala. It will pass after a few hours."

"This will really work?" Mackenzie asked as Maigret placed a small pouch in her hands.

"Aye, it will," said Maigret. "Be brave, lass. You're not alone." She squeezed Mackenzie's arm and turned to Finian. "She's in your care again until tomorrow night. Mind that she doesn't come to any harm."

"I don't suppose you have any idea the risk the old woman is taking, helping you and your sister," Finian said to Mackenzie as he rowed them back to land. "Faeries like Nuala aren't pleasant when they're crossed."

Mackenzie's hands were clenched in her lap. She kept her eyes fixed on the dark shoreline. "So why does Maigret do it then? Who is she?"

"She *was* a lass just like you, lured down here by one of Nuala's kind many years ago with a bit of faery gold. There was no one to warn her otherwise, so she drank from the cup and had to serve a faery mistress for seven years. She was freed at the end of that time, but when she returned to the world above, everything had changed. Seven years in the land below was more than seventy in the world above. The seasons turn at different speeds above and below. Except at the solstices, when the two worlds brush against each other."

Something broke the surface of the water a few yards away. Mackenzie tensed.

"Just a fish," said the piper, still rowing.

"What did Maigret do?" Mackenzie asked, breathing again.

"There was naught for her in the world above. She was a stranger there. Everyone she loved had passed. So she found her way back down to this world."

Mackenzie waited as Finian steered the boat next to the low wharf. He tied the line around a post and climbed out.

"But why?" she asked when he offered his hand. "Why come back here?"

Finian grunted. "Isn't it obvious? To save others from the same fate."

"Like me and my sister," said Mackenzie.

"Aye," said Finian. "Lassies, laddies—she's got a soft place in her heart for all of you. Soft place in her head, more like. Of course, she's not the only one scouring the edges for stray bairns at this time of year. 'Tis a race every time to see if she can hide one or two. 'Tis a shame some of you don't have the sense to stay hidden," he added darkly.

Mackenzie followed the piper from the wharf onto the shore. "What about you?" she asked, trying to keep her voice neutral. "You're not here to save anyone, are you? I mean, it's your music that puts people into a trance so they'll drink from the cup."

Finian stopped abruptly, his arms stiff at his side. Even in the dark, Mackenzie could see the lines of his face hardening. "I don't lure anyone here. I don't lift the cup to anyone's lips."

"I-I'm sorry," Mackenzie said after a moment.

The two baskets of clothing were still in the recess where Mackenzie and her sister had hidden them. "Do you have a knife I can borrow?" Mackenzie asked.

"Of course." Finian produced a small knife from a sheath under his cloak and handed it to her. "Sometimes a good blade is the only thing a Pooka understands."

"Thanks." Mackenzie pulled two pairs of jeans and two sweaters from the baskets. She cut a few inches of fabric from the hems of the jeans and cut off half an arm from each sweater. "I hope this is enough," she said as she handed the pieces to Finian, who tucked them away in a pouch. She stuffed what was left of the clothing back into the baskets and hid them again.

"Let's get moving," said the piper. "The sky is getting lighter. Day will be breaking shortly."

Breanne was still unresponsive when Mackenzie returned to their room. Mackenzie sat down beside her sister and took her hand. "Can you hear me, Breanne?"

When she didn't answer, Mackenzie went on anyway. "I went to see Maigret—remember the old woman who found us in the marsh? She's helping us. We're going to break you free from this spell. You just have to hang on," Mackenzie whispered, as much to herself as her sister. "Everything is going to be all right, I promise."

CHAPTER ELEVEN

Mackenzie's eyes fluttered a few times and then flew open as they registered the figure standing beside the bed.

"I've disturbed you," said Nuala. "And you were sleeping so soundly."

"I-I was awake most of the night. Watching my sister," Mackenzie added quickly.

Nuala tilted her head toward Breanne. "I told you to stop worrying about her. Look at the peaceful expression on her face. The fever is almost gone. She'll be awake soon."

Mackenzie nodded nervously. She didn't meet the faery's eyes. "That's good, I guess."

"Of course it is. But it was you I came to see," the faery said, pulling back the blankets that covered

Mackenzie's body. "There's a *fidchell* tournament today, and I need an extra player."

"But I don't even know what *fidchell* is."

"I'll teach you," said the faery.

"But Breanne—" Mackenzie turned to look at her sister.

"No excuses this time," said Nuala, crossing her slender arms. "I need a player, and you need a diversion. Let's get you dressed quickly."

Nuala explained the rules of *fidchell* as they traveled to the surface of the mound, but they didn't make much sense to Mackenzie in her sleep-deprived state. She was given a white headdress in the shape of a dove's head as soon as they reached the area where the tournament was being held. Nuala led her into position on a circular terrace. There were at least two dozen other humans wearing dove headdresses on the terrace, and the same number with the black beaks and feathers of ravens. Except for Mackenzie, they all shared the blank faces of the solstice-bound.

The object of the white team, as much as Mackenzie understood it, was to form a continuous line from a marker at the center of the terrace out to the last of seven concentric circles formed by paving stones. The object of the black team was to make this impossible. It didn't take Mackenzie long to figure out that the humans weren't really players but game pieces on a giant board. Their role was to remain perfectly still until commanded to move. It was the faeries strolling around the terrace who strategized and made decisions.

The game moved slowly from the beginning, and the intervals between moves grew longer as it progressed. It might have enthralled the faeries playing the game, but it was agony for Mackenzie. She had to dig her nails into her palms to prevent herself from falling asleep on her feet. In the end, even that wasn't enough.

Mackenzie's eyes flew open. Something hard had rapped against her wrist. "I'm sorry!" she said quickly.

"I *said*, 'Advance!'" said Nuala, her silver eyes flashing angrily.

Mackenzie scurried clockwise to the next space in the circle.

"Not there, *there*," said Nuala. She pointed the slender rod in her hand to another space, to the right of where Mackenzie had been standing.

"I'm sorry," Mackenzie repeated, her face going crimson. She stumbled on a loose paving stone on her way to the new position and had to pick herself up.

Nuala glared at Mackenzie as two of the faeries on the other team began to laugh behind their hands. She called out something in her own language, and one of the white players who'd been "captured" earlier and removed from the board came to take Mackenzie's place.

"Go. Go!" said Nuala, shooing Mackenzie and the attendant who'd come up beside her away. "Get some sleep before the banquet. You're useless to me like this."

❧

Nuala was in a better mood when she swept into Mackenzie's room several hours later. "Wake up—it's time to get ready! Look what I brought for you this evening. Do you see how it catches the light? You won't find silk like *this* anywhere in your world."

Mackenzie sat up groggily and rubbed her eyes. Two attendants were advancing with a single gown stretched out between them. The first girl released the lower half of the dress, and half a dozen layers of filmy, translucent fabric fluttered slowly to the ground.

"It's pretty," said Mackenzie, still half asleep.

Nuala made a pouting face as she flounced down in a chair across the room. "It's pretty—that's all you can say about it? I was hoping for a little more enthusiasm. But I suppose you're still brooding about your sister."

The faery held up her palms before Mackenzie could answer. "I know, I know," she said with an impatient sigh. "You're afraid your sister will wake up, and you won't be here to help her. But Deirdre will stay with her, won't you, Deirdre?" she said as her red-haired servant advanced to stand by the foot of the bed. "She won't leave the room until you return."

The faery clapped her hands. "Now that that's settled, let's forget your sister for a little while, shall we? Try on the dress. You'll forget your own name when you feel that silk against your skin."

❧

Mackenzie had accompanied Nuala all the way to the entrance of the courtyard before she realized she'd forgotten something even more important than her name. She stopped abruptly, her hands flying to the empty folds of the thin gown under her cloak. She hadn't brought a single bogberry.

A faery with fox ears hissed angrily as he collided with her. "I'm sorry," Mackenzie squeaked, leaping quickly out of his way.

"What's wrong with you?" Nuala asked as she turned and waited for Mackenzie to catch up. "You've gone as pale as a water nymph."

"I-I—" Mackenzie searched her mind frantically for an excuse to go back.

"Well?"

Mackenzie's panicked mind had gone blank. "I'm fine," she said faintly.

The banquet that evening was even wilder than it had been the night before. As the revelry reached a drunken pitch, none of the assembled guests seemed to notice the animals eating freely off the tables. Mackenzie recoiled as a mouse scurried past her plate. A hawk swooped down a moment later and took the mouse in a single bite. Mackenzie didn't even pretend to take an interest in the food in front of her. Her knuckles were white in her lap. With the arrival of each new course, she became more desperate to get away.

Out of the corner of her eye, she watched Nuala and the other faeries farther down the table laugh with a savage excitement. Nuala's head was thrown back, and her cheeks were flushed with wine and exhilaration.

Mackenzie eased herself back from the table while Nuala was still distracted. She gathered her skirts. She was just half an inch above her seat when a hand closed around her wrist.

"Where are you going?" Nuala asked, her eyes narrowing.

"I-I was just going to stretch my legs," Mackenzie whispered.

"But you haven't touched the wine in your cup. And look, the piper has arrived to play for us." The faery tightened her fingers, and Mackenzie felt a small shock travel up her arm. "Stay," Nuala said sweetly, an icy smile on her face.

Mackenzie's stomach churned as she watched Finian settle himself at the center of the courtyard. Every muscle in her body was tensed as if waiting for a blow.

The first notes were soft, teasing. If they had stayed that way, Mackenzie was sure she could have resisted them. But the music didn't remain gentle. It swelled quickly until it was a crushing wave of sound. Mackenzie did everything she could to resist it. She bit the insides of her cheeks until they were raw. She chewed on her tongue. Her fingernails left bloody imprints where they cut into her palms.

She forgot about Nuala's presence beside her. There was only the piper's music and her struggle against it. She covered her ears and buried her head in her lap, but it was still there, ringing in her head, battering her body.

She felt the air explode around her. It was like an enormous electric pulse, making every hair on her body stand on end. Her head throbbed. When the pipes fell silent at last, she thought her eardrums had ruptured. Several seconds passed before she could summon the courage to sit up and open her eyes.

The struggle had cost Mackenzie all of her strength. She could barely hold herself upright as the solstice cup was carried toward her at the front of the faery procession. The cup itself was a blur: two cups, three cups, coming closer and closer. Nuala steadied her as Mackenzie accepted the vessel with both hands.

"Drink," the faery whispered.

Mackenzie was too tired to resist. She let Nuala guide the cup to her mouth. Her lips parted…

At the last possible second she heard the pipes again, one soft note that was gone as soon as it had begun, as if she'd only imagined it. She hesitated and then tilted the cup again.

The liquid reached her lips, but her lips were closed. She swallowed her own saliva twice and let Nuala take the cup back. She didn't have to fake the tremor that went through her body.

CHAPTER TWELVE

Anger had given Mackenzie some of her strength back when Finian showed up at the doorway of her room later that night.

"Are you ready?" the piper called softly into the darkened chamber.

"Why—why do you do it?" she demanded, sputtering in her rage. "My mouth is bloody—it's a mess! I can barely talk because of you—you and that *music*! And my sister—" Mackenzie's voice faltered as she turned to the bed, where Breanne was still asleep. "How can you be their Pied Piper, leading people right into their trap? How can you be so—so *evil*?"

Finian was silent for almost a full minute. When he spoke again, his voice was ice. "There are some things wee lassies like you could never begin to understand.

I've helped you and your sister repeatedly, and I'll take you to the old woman now if you're ready. But I won't explain myself to you."

"I don't need your help," Mackenzie said, her heart thundering. "I can find my way myself."

The piper snorted. "Oh, you can, can you? Then by all means." With an awkward flourish, he gestured toward the hallway.

"I know the way," Mackenzie insisted.

"I do not doubt it. But does the way know you?"

"What are you talking about?"

Finian stood aside. "Find out for yourself. But let me warn you—you won't get far. The passageways will be short, and they won't lead you anywhere. You'll find many walls and few doorways, and then you'll find no doorways at all. If luck favors you, you might find your way back here. Then again, you might not."

Mackenzie remained silent.

"Let me know what you decide," Finian said. "I'm at your service."

With an effort, Mackenzie brought her voice under control. "If you won't tell me why you're helping faeries like Nuala trap people, will you at least tell me why you're bothering to help me and my sister?"

"It's not you I'm helping. I told you, I owe a debt to Maigret."

"So how come you can come and go as you please?" Mackenzie asked, her arms crossed. "Why do the hallways stay open for you?"

"The ways are charmed against those the faeries don't trust. They trust me, of course. I've earned certain privileges for my faithful service."

"I'll bet," Mackenzie muttered as she looked down at Breanne's still form on the bed a few feet away. She uncrossed her arms. "All right. If you're my only way back to Maigret tonight, I guess—I guess we'd better get going."

"There's a bright lass," said the piper.

❧

Mackenzie didn't speak to her escort as she trailed a few feet behind him, not even when they were out of the faery mound and well on their way to the water. Finian untied the same boat they'd used the night before, and they rowed across to Maigret's shack in silence.

"There you are, delivered in one piece," the piper said, nodding at the ladder that led up into the shack. "You know the plan. I'll be back before dawn."

"Thank you," Mackenzie said stiffly.

"Wait—you've forgotten something."

From underneath his cloak, Finian pulled the pouch that held the fragments of cloth from

Mackenzie's and Breanne's clothing. He tossed it across the boat. Mackenzie picked it up and started up the ladder.

Maigret was waiting at the top. "Come in, lass, come in," she said as she took Mackenzie's arm and led her across the dim, lamp-lit space. "The loom is ready. You brought the pieces of cloth from your own garments?"

"They're right here." Mackenzie held up the pouch.

"Good. I spent the day spinning fibers from the marsh into twine—enough to get you started."

The old woman positioned Mackenzie in front of the empty loom, which consisted of four wooden poles lashed together at the corners to form a tall frame that leaned against the wall. Two narrower poles were attached by slender ropes to the bottom and top poles.

"You have to string the warp threads to start—the ones that go from top to bottom," Maigret said. She handed Mackenzie a ball of very coarse yarn.

"Wouldn't it be easier if you did this part?" Mackenzie asked as she struggled to follow Maigret's directions. The yarn was supposed to wind continuously from the bottom pole to the top one and back again, forming tight parallel lines across the loom. Mackenzie kept dropping the ball of yarn as she traced clumsy figure eights around each pole.

"Keep the yarn taut," Maigret said. "That's it. Aye, it would be easier for me to do the whole thing. But the weaving must be all yours, or the mantle's power against Nuala's magic will be diluted. It's enough that I did the spinning."

When the warp threads were in place, Maigret directed Mackenzie to insert a long stick between every other thread. "That's your shed stick, to keep the warp threads open. Now the batten." She handed Mackenzie a flat stick with a sharpened edge and instructed her to insert it under the shed stick. "There, that gives you room for the shuttle."

Mackenzie took the long flat stick with yarn wrapped around it and began weaving it through the warp threads, releasing yarn from it as she went. It was a painstaking process, even with the batten in place to hold the warp threads open for the shuttle. Following Maigret's directions, she used a wooden comb to pack down the weft threads she'd just woven in.

Mackenzie surveyed her progress and then tensed her body in frustration. "It's a mess!"

"It's not a silk dress you're weaving, lass." Maigret put a wrinkled hand on Mackenzie's arm. "It doesn't matter what it looks like."

"But there's no way I can weave a whole cloak by the day after tomorrow. It's impossible!"

"'Tis a mantle, not a cloak. It doesn't have to be big. It just needs to be wide enough to cover your sister's shoulders. Keep going," Maigret urged. "Don't think about it—just do it. Your fingers will learn. Soon enough they'll be flying across the loom."

Mackenzie closed her eyes and tried to breathe deeply, but her chest was too tight. "I can't do this. It's too much!"

The old woman released her arm. "You might as well give up then. This is an easy task compared to the next one."

"But I can't just leave my sister here," Mackenzie said, her voice cracking. "How could I?"

Maigret didn't answer.

Mackenzie took another breath and picked up the shuttle. "All right," she said as she squeezed it in her fist. "I'll weave a mantle."

❧

Mackenzie lost track of time as she concentrated on moving the shuttle in and out of the warp threads, back and forth across the loom. She'd completed a rough strip of fabric approximately two inches high by three feet long when Finian appeared at the top of the ladder to ferry her back to the island.

"But I've barely started," Mackenzie protested as she rose reluctantly from her stool.

"You've done well for your first time, lass," Maigret said. "It will go faster tomorrow night."

"What about the pieces from our clothes?"

"You'll weave them in tomorrow," said the old woman. She put her hand on Mackenzie's shoulder and steered her away from the loom. "You have to go with Finian now. You've got to be back in your chamber before first light. Have you still got the herbs I gave you last night?

"Good," she said when Mackenzie nodded. "Take half of them in a wee bit of water just before you lie down. You'll be hot as a burning ember in no time. Nuala will never know you didn't drink from the cup last night. She'll leave you alone after she's felt your skin, and you can sleep for the rest of the day.

"Do get some sleep, child," Maigret called softly as Mackenzie descended the ladder after Finian. "You'll need your rest come tomorrow night."

Breanne was still asleep when Mackenzie got back to their room, but her body had cooled considerably. "We're almost out of here," Mackenzie whispered as she squeezed her sister's hand. "Just one more night to get through, that's it."

Breanne's eyes opened a crack.

"Are you awake?" Mackenzie said eagerly.

Breanne blinked twice, and then her eyelids dropped again.

"All right," said Mackenzie. "You're still tired, but that's okay. I don't know if you can hear me, but I'm going to join you in bed for a little while."

As she spoke, Mackenzie poured half the herb mixture Maigret had given her into a cup of water and swirled it around. She lifted the cup to her nose and grimaced. "This stuff smells disgusting! I can't tell you how much I wish you were here," she said to Breanne as she got ready to take the first sip. "I mean *really* here. You've got ten times the courage I have. It's true—I'm a wuss compared to you."

She tilted the cup, gagging as the bitter concoction reached her tongue. She had to force herself to swallow.

"I've been following you everywhere since kindergarten," she whispered to her sister between sips. "No, make that since we could crawl. I'd be lost if something happened to you."

When the cup was empty, Mackenzie lifted the covers and climbed into bed. "I don't know how long it's been since I said this, but—I love you, Breanne."

Mackenzie was barely aware of Nuala's presence when the faery came to check on her later that morning. She felt something brush her forehead, but she was too tired to open her eyes. The fever Maigret had promised was not nearly as painful as Mackenzie had feared. It was like lying on a hot sandy beach beneath a tropical sun. The ebb and flow of her breath became the ebb and flow of gentle waves, lulling her to sleep. She let herself drift.

The room was lit by a single candle when Mackenzie woke up. The fever had left her body, and her mind was clear, but she had no idea how much time had passed. She remained in bed beside her sister, in case Nuala or one of the faery's attendants came to check on them. She let herself doze off again until she heard Finian call softly from the hallway.

Breanne's hand closed around her wrist before she could rise from the bed. "You're awake!" Mackenzie whispered.

Breanne's eyes shone palely in the candlelight. Her mouth moved as if she were speaking, but nothing came out.

"Are you okay?" Mackenzie asked anxiously. "Can you speak?"

Breanne's lips moved again, but there was still no sound. Her eyes widened in alarm as she raised her free hand to her throat.

"We have to go," Finian called from the hallway.

"Wait! Let me at least get my sister some water," said Mackenzie. She found a pitcher of water and a cup and brought them back to the bed. Breanne was as weak as a newborn. Mackenzie had to lift her sister's head and hold the cup to her lips while she drank.

"It's all right, Bree," Mackenzie said when her sister was finished. "It's going to be okay—I promise. But I have to go now. I don't have time to explain. I'll be back in a few hours."

She peeled her sister's fingers from her wrist and moved away from the bed. "I'm really sorry, but I have to do this," she said as she backed toward the door, away from her sister's pleading eyes. "I *am* coming back. And tomorrow night we can both ditch this place for good."

Mackenzie and Finian traveled in silence all the way down to the shore. The piper was the first to speak, as he untied the small rowboat from the wharf. "You're a rare one, you know that?" he said as he prepared to push off through the dark water. "They're not like you, the others who come here chasing faery gold. You think it's my music that makes them drink and keeps them in the land below?"

He paused to spit over the side of the boat.

"Feeble-minded bairns. They see the twinkling lights, the faeries on parade in their pretty costumes. They eat faery food and sleep on feather beds. The wee laddies and lassies are spellbound long before they hear my pipes. You think they want to leave? They'd sell their kin to stay!"

"To be slaves for seven years?" Mackenzie asked angrily. "Does anyone explain that part to them?"

Finian kept his voice low as he rowed, but his tone was bitter. "They don't know the difference. They're fed well; they're clothed. Even Nuala doesn't mistreat her human attendants. Where's the harm in a few years of service?"

"Where's the harm? Where's the *harm*?" Mackenzie sputtered. "What about when they go home again, and everyone they love is old or dead?"

Finian lifted the oars and they drifted toward the pilings that supported Maigret's shack. "It's not always like that," he said defensively. "Sometimes only a season has passed. Sometimes only a few days."

"Sometimes?" Mackenzie stared at the dark outline of the piper's face and shook her head. "You warned us not to drink from the cup from the very beginning, when Breanne found that piece from your pipes in the hallway. You warned us, and you've tried to protect us, because you *know* what the solstice cup does is wrong. It's evil!"

"'Twas only a favor for the old woman," said Finian.

The boat bumped against a piling. The piper nodded curtly at the ladder above their heads. "We're here."

"Well?" he said when Mackenzie didn't immediately step out of the boat. "Go on then. You don't want to keep her waiting."

"This conversation isn't over," said Mackenzie.

CHAPTER THIRTEEN

"I don't get it," Mackenzie blurted the instant she was through Maigret's trapdoor. "You help people escape from faeries like Nuala, right? So why do you trust Finian? He's working for them! It's *his* music that puts people into a trance. *He's* the reason people drink from the solstice cup, no matter what he says!"

The old woman took both of Mackenzie's hands and held them firmly. "Take a deep breath."

"Breanne wouldn't be a zombie if it wasn't for Finian's stupid pipes! I wouldn't have to weave a mantle to rescue her—we could both just leave tomorrow night!"

"Breathe," Maigret repeated.

"I am breathing," Mackenzie said as she yanked her hands away. "But I don't understand any of this, and I'm *angry*!"

"Aye, and if that's what you bring to the loom tonight, you might as well go right back down that ladder. The mantle will have no power if it's woven through with bitterness."

Mackenzie's chin dropped to her chest. She wrapped her arms around her body and began to sob.

Maigret's voice softened. "There, there, lass," she said as she embraced the shuddering girl. "That's right, let the tears fall. You've every right to be upset."

"I'm all right," Mackenzie said after a moment, wiping her eyes and pulling gently away.

"Good." The old woman nodded. "Then you'd best get started."

❧

The weaving went faster this time. Mackenzie's hands became more nimble until the shuttle was flying back and forth across the loom as Maigret had promised. The weft threads accumulated, one on top of another. The woven fabric was four inches high, then it was six inches, then eight.

The old woman was a silent presence seated on a basket off to one side of the loom. Mackenzie had almost forgotten that she was there until Maigret leaned forward to inspect the coarse fabric. "'Tis good work. You've a knack for this."

Mackenzie stretched her back and rubbed her sore fingers. "Thank you."

"Aye, 'tis very good." The old woman patted Mackenzie on the shoulder and stepped back.

"You asked why I have anything to do with Finian," Maigret said when Mackenzie's hands were traveling across the loom again. "He's not my kin, but I feel as responsible for him as you feel for your sister."

Mackenzie stopped and turned, but Maigret motioned her to continue.

"He followed me here when he was just a youth, Finian did," said Maigret. "He heard me telling stories in the village when I'd first returned from my seven years of service. That's what the villagers thought they were, the stories of a crazy woman. None of them knew me. Too many years had passed above ground, and all my kin were dead. They mocked me, the villagers. All of them save the youth with the humped back. He believed, young Finian did. He asked me to lead him down to the Otherworld, tried to buy his way with a little flute he'd whittled from an ash branch. 'Twas the only thing of value he possessed."

"And you brought him here?" said Mackenzie as she finished another row.

The old woman shrugged her shoulders. "I would never knowingly have led anyone to this place. When I came back, it was to save others from repeating my fate. There was nothing left for me in the world above—that became plainer every day I was there. The only person who had time for me was Finian, and only because his deformity made him an outcast too. I couldn't return right away. I had to wait for the next solstice. And all the while Finian begged me to take him to the faeries. 'Twas an obsession with him."

"Why?" asked Mackenzie. "What did he want from them?"

"He wanted to be looked at without revulsion," said Maigret. "Like other men."

"But his back is still deformed."

"Aye, but you're getting ahead of the story." Maigret cleared her throat. "I had been staying in a ruined hut a little ways from the village. To evade Finian, who slept under a rock ledge nearby, I rose before daybreak the morning of the summer solstice. I crept away quietly and went to the wee creek where I'd spied the faery ring so many years past. But the ring wasn't there. The sun rose higher and higher in the sky as I searched the bank. I kept looking, even when the light started to fade again. It wasn't until dusk that what I sought appeared at last, a bit of gold gleaming at the water's edge. I went to it and picked it up, and immediately someone leapt out of the bushes from above. It was Finian—he'd followed me from the hut. He grabbed my arm and held on to it as we were both pulled into the water and carried away."

Mackenzie had stopped weaving, caught up in Maigret's story. She waited as the old woman paused to take a breath.

"I was angry—as angry as you were when you arrived tonight. I begged Finian to hide with me in the edges—in the marshes that surround the faeries' world—to wait with me until the ways opened again and he could go home. But he would not wait. He found his way to the island and presented himself to the fair folk at once. He made his request, and he was promised that his back would be fixed if he drank from the solstice cup at the end of the banquet that night."

"But it's not," Mackenzie argued.

"Nay, he didn't drink from the cup after all," said Maigret. "Finian had brought his wooden flute with him, and the faeries saw it as they were feasting that night. They asked him to play a tune for them— faeries love good music. Finian's flute was a humble instrument, but he played it well. So well that they brought out a set of faery pipes next and asked him to play those too." The old woman's voice grew hushed. "You've heard the music Finian makes with those pipes. He has a rare talent."

"It—it's evil, his music," said Mackenzie. "It puts some kind of spell on people."

"On Finian too," said Maigret. "You know what it does to you and your sister when you listen without protection. Imagine the effect it's had on Finian, playing that music season after season. He won't eat any bogberries to protect himself. It's like a sickness— he's come to love that music more than food or air."

"He should destroy the pipes," Mackenzie said angrily. "He knows that people drink from the solstice cup because they're too stunned by his music to refuse it."

"A mother could as soon destroy her babe as Finian could destroy those pipes," Maigret said with an impatient shake of her head. "Aye, the pipe's music enchants everyone who hears it, unless they've eaten bogberries first. But you must understand—visitors to this world were drinking from the solstice cup long before Finian arrived. Faeries like Nuala would find another way to make them take the cup if Finian was ever to leave. He's not the enemy, lass."

"So what happened?" said Mackenzie. "You said Finian was going to drink from the cup, but then he didn't."

"The fair folk wouldn't let him have it," Maigret said. "Not once they'd heard him play. It takes feeling, a unique awareness of the world, to produce that kind of music. You've seen the other human attendants. They're mute. Their emotions are blunted. They're like sleepwalkers. Finian's gift would have been lost had he drunk from the solstice cup like the others. The faeries wouldn't let that happen. They wanted the music to continue. So they found another way to bind the young musician to them. They let him keep the pipes—with one condition."

"That he stayed in their world and played for them," Mackenzie finished.

"Aye, Finian is bound to the fair folk as surely as if he'd drunk from that cup."

Mackenzie was silent as she digested the old woman's story. "I don't see why you feel responsible for him. It was his decision to follow you here."

Maigret shook her head. "I should have taken more care. I knew he'd try to follow, and yet I came anyway."

"Finian says he owes you for something," said Mackenzie. "That you did him a favor."

"He counts it a favor that I led him here, unwitting gift that it was," Maigret said with a grunt. "He was nothing in the world he came from. He was a wretch, an outcast. Here he has the pipes, and the respect and admiration their music brings."

"The respect and admiration of the faeries, maybe. He doesn't care what happens to the *people* who hear his music," Mackenzie said darkly.

"It pains him more than he lets show," Maigret said as she stood up. "But that's enough about Finian. 'Tis your sister's plight we need to think about now." She picked up the pouch that held the pieces of fabric Mackenzie had cut from her and her sister's clothing. "Time to weave these in."

Under the old woman's direction, Mackenzie tore the fabric into narrower strips. She knotted them together to form one long strip, which she wound around the shuttle.

"Aye, that's it," said Maigret as Mackenzie wove the fabric strips through the taut warp threads. When Mackenzie had used up all the fabric, she reloaded the shuttle with the coarse twine Maigret had spun for her.

"I have one more question," Mackenzie said before she started weaving again. "Why is Finian still young, if you've—"

"Become an ancient crone?" Maigret finished with a smile. "This is the land of eternal youth. At least it is for those eating faery food every day, like Finian. But I eat only what I gather and prepare with my own hands."

"I see," said Mackenzie.

The movement of the shuttle back and forth across the loom was hypnotic. Mackenzie was only vaguely aware of her stiffening muscles and the blisters forming on her fingertips. Without a way to track the passage of time as she worked, Finian's arrival caught her by surprise.

"Ready?" the piper called from the trapdoor. "'Tis past time we were off."

"But I'm not finished," Mackenzie said, turning to Maigret in dismay. "It's not nearly big enough yet!"

"'Twill have to suffice as it is," said Maigret. "Finian's right, lass. You've run out of time." She gently pried the shuttle from Mackenzie's hands and replaced it with a bone needle threaded with more coarse yarn. "You need to stitch up the edges of your weaving so they don't unravel. That's right," she said as Mackenzie began to sew. "Big stitches—they don't have to be even."

"'Twill be light soon," Finian said impatiently. "I can't wait much longer."

"I'm working as fast as I can," said Mackenzie.

"Now listen to me carefully," Maigret said when the hemming was finished and the rectangle of fabric had been removed from the loom. She gripped Mackenzie by the shoulders and looked sternly into her eyes. "There is one more thing you must do before the weaving is complete. The mantle is a counter-charm against the magic of the solstice cup. It has pieces from your sister's clothing to return her to herself and pieces from your clothing to bind your sister to you until you're both away."

Mackenzie nodded nervously.

"But the charm is incomplete until you add one more element—a fiber from one of Nuala's garments."

Mackenzie felt the blood drain from her face. "But—how do I get that?" she asked faintly.

Maigret's gray eyes didn't waver. "You must rip it out. A bit of thread will do." She pressed the bone needle into Mackenzie's hand. "When you have it, you must sew it into the mantle."

"How am I supposed to do that?" Mackenzie asked, her throat constricting. "I don't know where Nuala's room is! I don't know where she keeps her clothes!"

"Then you must take it from the garment she is wearing," said Maigret. "Bite one of your fingernails so that it's ragged, and use it to snag her gown as she leans over you."

Mackenzie could barely hear the old woman over the blood rushing through her head.

"You must keep the mantle out of sight until the last moment," Maigret continued, ignoring the dismay on Mackenzie's face. "Fold it up and hide it under the shift you wear under your dress. You and your sister will be led outside at nightfall for the Sealing Ceremony." She squeezed Mackenzie's arms gently. "Remember, Nuala believes you've drunk from the cup. No matter what you see, you can't give yourself away until it's time."

"When do I bring out the mantle?" Mackenzie managed to say through clenched teeth.

"When your sister steps into the fire," Maigret replied. "Not a moment sooner. Throw it over her shoulders, and then hold on tight. You must hold on with every bit of courage and strength you have.

Nuala will fight to keep your sister, but she cannot harm you once you've crossed into the fire. Whatever you see, whatever you hear, it's all an illusion. Remember that, lass."

CHAPTER FOURTEEN

There was a faint glow all around the horizon when Mackenzie left Maigret's shack. She hurried down the ladder after Finian and stepped into the rowboat that waited below.

"We'll have to move like the wind itself," the piper muttered as he started rowing. "We've dallied too long on this side of the water."

Mackenzie clutched the folded mantle to her chest and said nothing.

When they reached the opposite shore, Finian secured the boat with a hasty knot and strode off. Mackenzie had to take the stairs two at a time to keep up with him. She was out of breath before they'd even reached the end of the first avenue.

There was no sunrise, only a gradual softening of the darkness, like black ink fading to gray. The twisted silhouettes around them became ghostly trees and thorn bushes. As they turned onto the path that led up to the faery mound, Mackenzie heard small scurrying noises in the undergrowth.

"You'd best move those legs faster," Finian called over his shoulder. "There are creatures out here that wake with an appetite."

Mackenzie didn't need any more urging. She caught up with the piper immediately and stayed by his side until they were underground.

Finian put his finger to his lips as they entered the first torch-lit passage. He pulled Mackenzie into a dark alcove and whispered in her ear. "Most faeries will still be in bed, but it would only take one to raise the alarm. Stay with me, and if I squeeze your arm, freeze. Don't even breathe. Do you understand?"

Mackenzie nodded.

The distance between the entrance to the faery mound and Mackenzie's chamber seemed twice as long this time. She couldn't even be sure that Finian was taking the same route he'd used the previous two nights. In the dim light, every passage looked the same. She held her breath as they approached each turn. Halfway down a long corridor she heard the sound she'd been dreading: footsteps approaching from a side passage.

Finian pulled her backward so quickly that she nearly lost her balance. He shoved her through the nearest doorway. He was halfway through after her when a woman's voice called out to him.

"Is that you, Piper? You're out of bed early."

Mackenzie froze.

"Aye, 'tis me, my lady," Finian said, backing out into the hallway again. "I couldn't sleep. I've been composing something special for tonight's ceremony."

Mackenzie heard suspicion in the faery's voice. "Do you always compose so far from your chamber?"

"Indeed, my lady," Finian said smoothly. "My best pieces always come to me as my feet are wandering. And may I ask why you are awake so early this morning?"

"It's not early—it's late," the faery said with a girlish laugh. "I haven't been to bed yet. Perhaps you could escort me there and play a simple tune to put me to sleep."

From the shadows, Mackenzie saw Finian give a gallant bow. "Nothing would please me more."

❧

"He's coming back," Mackenzie told herself as she waited, crouched down in an empty room with Breanne's mantle pressed to her chest. "He has to come back." Her ears strained for the sound of approaching footsteps, but the corridor outside remained silent.

"Come on, where are you, Finian?"

She gave him ten minutes, until the count of six hundred. She gave him five minutes more, and then five after that. By the time it added up to half an hour, she was too anxious to sit any longer.

"I can find the way," Mackenzie told herself as she reentered the hallway. "I go straight, and then I turn left—"

Any confidence she had evaporated at the end of the corridor. There was a junction, but both arms of the T ended abruptly at blank walls. Mackenzie retraced her steps. There was an entrance to another passage just down from the room where she'd waited for Finian. She followed it several yards until it led around a corner—and she found herself dead-ended again.

Mackenzie hit the wall with her fist. "There *has* to be a way out," she said desperately.

She spun around at a rustling noise behind her. When a gray-hooded girl turned the corner with a large jug in her arms, she let out her breath. It was Deirdre, Nuala's redheaded attendant.

Mackenzie didn't wait for her heart to settle. "Please," she begged. "You have to help me! I need to get back, but all the hallways just end, like this one—" She turned to indicate the wall behind her, but it was no longer there. "What?" The corridor continued in a straight line as far as she could see.

"Right, the ways don't trust me. It opened for you." Mackenzie turned back to the servant, who had stopped a few paces away. "Please—I have to get to my room before Nuala gets there!"

The attendant's face remained impassive.

"Do you understand anything I'm saying?" Mackenzie asked, shaking her head in frustration. She started again, pronouncing each syllable carefully this time. "Are you going anywhere near my chamber? Because I could just follow if you are—"

She moved aside as she spoke, out of the attendant's path. The hooded girl came toward her and then walked past.

"I guess that's the best answer I'm going to get," said Mackenzie. "All right then, I'm right behind you."

⁂

They made it all the way to the corridor outside the chamber Mackenzie shared with her sister. Mackenzie's chest felt lighter the instant they turned the corner and she recognized the hallway. They were almost at the door—twenty paces away, then ten, then five—when Mackenzie heard an unmistakable jingling sound coming from an adjoining passage.

Half a dozen panicked thoughts raced through Mackenzie's mind as she swiveled to face the girl who'd been escorting her. In the split second that their eyes connected, Mackenzie thought she saw some emotion flicker across the attendant's face. She couldn't wait to find out for sure. She flew to her room, fumbling with the buttons of her outer garment as she ran.

Mackenzie was still pulling the gown over her head when she heard the sound of pottery shattering a short distance down the hall. Nuala's voice followed immediately, angry hisses and clicks that could only be curses. The distraction bought Mackenzie just enough time. She shoved the mantle under the mattress of the canopy bed and dove under the covers beside her sister. She had just chewed one of her fingernails to make it ragged when Nuala appeared at the door, still berating the girl in the hall.

Mackenzie left her hands above the quilted coverlet. She closed her eyes and prayed that her pounding heart and trembling limbs would pass for symptoms of the solstice fire she was supposed to have drunk two nights before.

She could hardly breathe as jingling footsteps approached the bed. There was a faint earthy smell, like a garden after a storm. Mackenzie felt a slight disturbance in the air above her face. It took all of her will not to flinch when the faery's fingers landed on her cheek.

"Are you dreaming of pretty things?" Nuala whispered as she stroked Mackenzie's skin. "I'm so glad you finally gave in."

Mackenzie forced herself to breathe evenly.

"And you," Nuala said, reaching past Mackenzie to Breanne. "I see your eyes fluttering, like moths still trapped in their cocoons. Don't worry—you won't be stuck in this bed much longer. I'll return this evening to help you both get up."

Mackenzie felt the silk of Nuala's wide sleeve trail over her hands. There was no time to think, no time to summon courage. She moaned softly and shifted position, as if she were stirring in her sleep. Her fingers scratched blindly at the fabric above them, and she felt a thread catch on her nail. "Please, oh please," she begged silently as her thumb joined her finger to tug at the tiny fiber. Her hand went limp a second later. She'd done as much as she dared.

An awful silence had fallen over the bed. Mackenzie made herself exhale as she waited to find out if she'd been discovered.

Inhale, exhale, slowly, deliberately.

She could hear her heart racing, could feel the sweat beading on her forehead. Just when she was sure her heart was going to explode, she heard the faery's voice.

"For a moment I thought you were awake," Nuala said softly. Her finger traced a path down Mackenzie's arm. "But of course you're not. You won't wake until I bring the herbs to rouse you this evening, will you?"

The faery's weight left the bed. "Until then, sleep tight, my sweet child."

⁘

Nuala had been gone for at least half an hour before Mackenzie felt safe enough to move. She raised her right hand toward the light of the nearest candle as she sat up carefully. What she saw between her finger and thumb made her so relieved that she shook her sister's shoulder.

"I got it! Oh, thank goodness—I got it! Let's hope it's enough."

It was a silver thread, barely a few inches long. Mackenzie held on to it carefully, hardly daring to breathe as she slid out of bed. With her free hand, she felt under the mattress for Breanne's mantle. Inside the folded mantle was a pouch with the needle Maigret had given her. She threaded the needle with the silver thread and stitched it into the coarse fabric of the mantle. There was enough thread to make a few tiny stitches, but not enough to knot it at the end.

Mackenzie surveyed her handiwork doubtfully. "It *has* to stay in." She shook her head and pulled the short thread out again. This time she knotted the thread around a single fiber and then used the blunt end of the needle to work the free ends of the thread into the weave on either side of the knot.

"That's better."

She pulled up the light shift she was wearing and wrapped the mantle around her waist so that it lay flat against her skin. She secured it with a slender piece of twine and pulled the shift back down again. The mantle was all but invisible beneath the loose undergarment.

After that, there was nothing Mackenzie could do but wait. She climbed into bed beside her sister and closed her eyes, with no expectation of sleep. Every muscle in her body was tense. Her mind stumbled down one anxious path after another.

In the end, exhaustion prevailed. Clinging to the top cover as if it were a life raft, Mackenzie drifted into a deep sleep not even dreams could reach.

CHAPTER FIFTEEN

Mackenzie woke retching. A sharp smell under her nose had pulled her back to consciousness.

"There, there," said a familiar voice. "You'll be fine in a moment."

Mackenzie blinked, trying to orient herself. The room was full of pale green light, as if somehow a bit of solstice fire had been brought inside. Nuala sat on the edge of the bed in a scarlet cloak. The hood of her cloak was raised so that only the lower half of her face was visible. Mackenzie saw a bundle of herbs disappear under the faery's cloak as Nuala withdrew her hand and stood up.

Mackenzie blinked again. Her mouth tasted metallic and she felt sluggish, as if she'd been drugged.

Her head pounded dully. It took her a few seconds to realize that it was not her pulse she could hear, but a drum beating somewhere deep in the faery compound.

She let one of Nuala's attendants help her out of bed. Behind her, she was vaguely aware of a second attendant assisting Breanne to her feet. Mackenzie raised her arms, and the first attendant slid a seamless white gown over her shift. The front of the dress's hem clung briefly to Mackenzie's undergarment at the level of her hips. It was only as the attendant was tugging it down, smoothing the bottom of the dress with her hands, that Mackenzie remembered the mantle hidden at her waist.

Her heart instantly accelerated. She was fully awake, all sluggishness gone. It was all she could do not to flee the room at the thought of how close she might have come to being discovered. As if the distant drummer could sense her agitation, the drumbeat got stronger and faster. Another drum joined the first, and then another one, until the room echoed with every muffled beat.

Nuala nodded her head, and the attendant who had clothed Mackenzie draped a white cloak over Mackenzie's shoulders. An identical cloak was wrapped around Breanne. Nuala nodded again, and her attendants each took a white-robed girl by the hand and led them to the door.

Mackenzie desperately wanted to look back at her sister as they traveled down the first hallway. Instead she forced herself to stare forward, to walk slowly and deliberately as if she were still in a trance. As the drums got more insistent, Mackenzie's fingers curled more tightly around the attendant's hand. Everything inside her felt clenched. She could barely breathe.

They reached the surface too quickly. Mackenzie couldn't help hesitating at the giant doorway. She had to take an extra half step to fall in stride with her escort again, but no one seemed to notice.

There were no tables in the courtyard this time. Instead, tiered stone seats rose to form an amphitheater. At the center was a huge faery bonfire, its green and white flames stretching like columns all the way to the sky.

Mackenzie didn't see the others dressed in white until they were only a few paces away. They stood in a silent circle around the bonfire, all but camouflaged against the pale, heatless flames. A moment later she was part of the circle, with Breanne beside her. The attendants slipped away.

Even with three layers covering her skin, Mackenzie felt naked under the piercing eyes of the faeries seated above her. She could almost feel their excitement, like static electricity in the air. It took all of her will to keep her expression blank, her feet rooted to the ground.

The drums beat one final frenzied tattoo and fell silent. The hair on Mackenzie's arms rose as a wild, keening cry went up from the faery host. It was a terrifying sound, like a gale-force wind howling over the glens, like a tribe of banshees wailing for a lost child.

Beneath the terrible chorus rose another sound. Out of the corner of her eye, Mackenzie saw Finian step forward into the circle around the bonfire, his pipes under his arm. He played a single sustained note that grew louder and louder until it had eclipsed the faery cry. When the last faery was silent, he began to play in earnest.

Mackenzie's limbs twitched involuntarily as the piper played. The music had an even stronger effect on the young woman in white standing to the piper's right. Her arms rose first to trace strange, jerky shapes in the air. Soon her whole body was twisting and contorting in a painful-looking dance. The movement carried her closer to the flames. Mackenzie didn't want to watch, but she couldn't turn away. She flinched when the young woman crossed over into the fire.

It was a horrible sight. The woman was a puppet to the relentless music. She was a rag doll tossed back and forth by the flames. Her spine arched, her limbs twisted at impossible angles. Her mouth opened wide in a silent scream.

Mackenzie wanted to throw up. She wanted to run to Finian and wrestle the pipes from his hands.

Her eyes slid to the piper, less than a dozen yards away. His eyes were closed, his expression unreadable. In the pale firelight, his skin looked gray.

There was a series of long notes, and the fire expelled the woman with a violent crack. Her white cloak had turned the color of ashes, the same color that all the faeries' attendants wore. No one came forward to help her when she fell in a heap.

Finian had to step around the still woman to reach the next person in the circle, a pale young man Mackenzie recognized from the first banquet. The nightmare process was repeated. The piper played, his victim danced, the fire expelled another one of the solstice-bound. It was the same every time. There were three young women between Finian and Breanne, then two, then one.

Under the cover of her cloak, Mackenzie fumbled with the string that secured the mantle around her body. She could feel the knots through the material of her dress. The first knot came undone easily, but the second was too tight. Her eyes remained locked on the piper as she struggled with the second knot.

He had finished with the last young woman.

He was moving.

He was standing beside Breanne.

Mackenzie's movements became more frantic, but it was already too late. Breanne's arms had risen. She had begun the awful lurching dance. Tears of anger and desperation appeared in Mackenzie's eyes. She yanked on the string beneath her dress, stumbling to her knees when it finally broke.

Breanne was inches away from the fire. Mackenzie grabbed the mantle, pulling it so quickly from her waist that it tore her skin. "Stop—can't you see what you're doing?" she screamed at Finian.

She was too occupied with the cloth in her hands to see the piper open his eyes. She didn't see the flicker of shame pass over his face, or see his fingers falter. There was a pause in the music, but Breanne had already crossed over into the pale flames. Mackenzie didn't see Nuala come up behind her either, as she plunged into the fire after her sister.

A jolt of electricity shot through Mackenzie's body when she threw the mantle over her sister's shoulders. There was a delay, like the pause between thunder and lightning, and then the pain registered. Mackenzie's head shot back and her face contorted, but she held on to her sister with a death grip. She held on as a third figure joined them in the flames, screaming with fury.

Nuala was almost unrecognizable in her anger. Mackenzie heard the faery hiss something, and Breanne thrashed and changed shape under Mackenzie's arms. She was a wild horse, bucking and braying while Mackenzie clung to her neck. She was a fox, snapping at Mackenzie's hands. She was an eagle with terrible talons and a vicious beak.

"It's all an illusion, it's all an illusion," Mackenzie repeated desperately to herself. She buried her face in her sister's shoulder and held on.

The feathers disappeared as Breanne changed again. Her torso stretched, becoming impossibly long. She was a sea serpent, thrashing and flailing. She was a dragon with razor-sharp scales that tore Mackenzie's clothing to shreds. Mackenzie's hands were raw and her muscles throbbed, but she would not let go. Even as she felt Breanne's flesh shift again, even as she heard Nuala howl, she knew she could hang on forever if she had to. She felt a wave of elation. She was going to win her sister back!

And then her sister's voice whimpered in her ear. "Let me go, Mackenzie! Please—you're burning me—*please* let go!"

Mackenzie opened her eyes. Breanne was back in her own body, but naked now. Angry welts had formed where the mantle rested against her skin. They began to blister and ooze even as Mackenzie watched. "Get it off me!" Breanne begged, tears streaming down her face.

Mackenzie felt her own eyes well up. "I can't, Bree. It will be over soon, I promise! You have to hang on!"

But it wasn't over soon. Breanne writhed in Mackenzie's arms, and her cries became more desperate. Mackenzie closed her eyes, but there was nothing she could do to escape her sister's screams.

They ricocheted back and forth in her skull. They pierced her brain so she couldn't think. They went on and on until Mackenzie couldn't take them anymore. She couldn't hold on. She had to let go—

Mackenzie heard a new sound just as she was about to release her sister. Finian was playing across a great distance, his music rising steadily until it was as loud as Breanne's howls. The pipes didn't block out the agony in Breanne's voice, but they softened it. Just enough—

Mackenzie tightened her grip around her sister's shoulders. She gritted her teeth and held on.

Everything fell silent.

The world went black.

CHAPTER SIXTEEN

Mackenzie was on her back in a boggy field, staring up at a leaden sky. She blinked as the first raindrop hit her face.

"W-we're soaked. We're completely drenched," she heard Breanne say through chattering teeth. "What happened? Did we go swimming with our clothes on?"

Mackenzie sat up carefully. "I don't know. I think we fell into a stream."

"I must have blacked out," said Breanne. "I had the weirdest dream."

Mackenzie swiveled to face her sister as the images in her head came into focus. She seized Breanne's arm. "You're okay! We made it back—both of us!"

"Back? Back from where?" Breanne asked warily.

"From the world below! From Nuala and the other faeries! We're *here*, Breanne! We're safe!"

Breanne shook her head and pulled away. "Uh-uh. No way was that real."

"It *was* real," Mackenzie said as she struggled to stand up. "Maigret, Finian, Nuala. You were there—you know what I'm talking about. I can see it in your eyes!"

Breanne was still shaking her head and looking at Mackenzie like she was crazy as she got to her feet. "I had a dream," she insisted. "A really weird dream. You heard me mumbling or something, and now you're trying to mess with my mind."

"It wasn't a dream—I can prove it." Mackenzie ran her hands down the sleeve of her jacket, and her voice faltered. "Except...I don't get why we're wearing our old clothes. This isn't what we were wearing when we left." She undid the wet jacket with some difficulty and slid one of her arms from its sleeve to inspect her sweater. "It doesn't make sense. I had to tear a piece off this sleeve to weave into your mantle. It was the only way I could free you after you drank from the solstice cup."

Breanne's face was flushed. "I don't know what you're talking about. *You* don't even know what you're talking about."

"Why are you so afraid of the truth?" said Mackenzie.

"You said you could prove it. So—prove it."

Mackenzie turned away in disgust. Her expression changed when she spied something sticking out of the mud a few feet away. She dropped to her knees, and within seconds she'd dug out a hollow piece of wood. The slender tube was already crumbling. The finger holes were barely discernible.

"Here—here's the proof," Mackenzie said triumphantly, holding it out.

Breanne snorted. "What's that supposed to be?"

"A piece from Finian's pipes! Don't tell me you don't remember Finian, because I know you do. Hey, where are you going?"

"To the farmhouse," Breanne said without looking back. "By the way? You've totally lost it."

Mackenzie watched her sister for several seconds before calling to her. "Hey! Breanne!"

"What?"

"You're not limping!"

❧

"So why didn't you let me go if I was screaming in pain?" Breanne asked later.

"Because I knew it was an illusion," said Mackenzie. "You weren't really being tortured."

"But how could you know that? How did you know you weren't burning my skin off with that mantle thing?"

"It had to be an illusion," Mackenzie said with a half smile. "You said 'please.' If you'd really been in pain, you would have been swearing at me."

It was ten thirty at night. The two sisters were in their beds in the guest room of the farmhouse. They'd found their way back just before dark, fifteen minutes before Uncle Eamon returned in his Land Rover. Aunt Joan had been beside herself when she'd seen the state of their clothes. They'd had to endure a tongue-lashing for leaving Cushendun and traveling cross-country on their own, but their only "punishment" was a mandatory half-hour soak for each of them. While Breanne sat in the bathtub, and Mackenzie sat beside her in an old washtub filled with heated water, Mackenzie told her sister everything that had happened after Breanne had drunk from the solstice cup. Breanne had remained skeptical throughout the evening, though she couldn't deny that her leg really was better.

Breanne shifted in her narrow cot. "So according to your version of events, what happened to the piper guy?"

"I don't know," said Mackenzie. "The solstice fire must have destroyed Finian's pipes when it transported us back here. Maybe the fire set Finian free too, sent him back to his own time. I hope he's all right, wherever he is. I would have let go of you if it hadn't been for his music at the end. He saved us, whether you believe any of this or not."

Breanne remained silent for a few seconds. "Look, I don't remember anything about solstice cups or evil faeries or any of that other stuff. But I do know you went into the water after me. So you can stop working the fantasy angle. I'm grateful, already."

Mackenzie's smile was hidden in the darkness. "So what are we going to do to kill time tomorrow?"

"I don't know. There's this cool ring somewhere out there that keeps slipping through my fingers. Want to look for it with me?"

"You're a real comedian, you know that, Breanne?" Mackenzie was still smiling as she drifted off to sleep.

ACKNOWLEDGMENTS

I couldn't write without the time, space and encouragement my family so generously provides. I am especially grateful to my husband, Bern, who helped fulfill a childhood dream when he applied for a teaching exchange that made it possible for our family to live in Northern Ireland for a year. For keen eyes and a clear voice, many thanks to my editor, Sarah Harvey.

RACHEL DUNSTAN MULLER is the author of two previous children's novels: *When the Curtain Rises* and *Ten Thumb Sam*. *The Solstice Cup* was conceived while Rachel was living on the northeastern shore of County Antrim, Northern Ireland. She currently lives on the edge of a small Vancouver Island community with her husband and five children.